Fatal Accusation

A Stein & Associates Thriller

Marian K. Riedy &
Tanja Steigner

Black Rose Writing | Texas

ISBN: 978-1-68433-467-4
PUBLISHED BY BLACK ROSE WRITING
www.blackrosewriting.com

Printed in the United States of America
Suggested Retail Price (SRP) $17.95

Fatal Accusation is printed in Sabon

*As a planet-friendly publisher, Black Rose Writing does its best to eliminate unnecessary waste to reduce paper usage and energy costs, while never compromising the reading experience. As a result, the final word count vs. page count may not meet common expectations.

Praise for

Fatal Accusation

A delightful thriller from authors Marian K. Riedy and Tanja Steigner, with a new twist on the old adage that "revenge is sweet." ~Cynthia Doroghazi, author of *Searching for the Open Door: A Woman's Struggle for Survival after a Traumatic Brain Injury*

Textured and nuanced, this fast-paced legal thriller will engage and entertain. From the gates of Hell to the gates of the NSA, Riedy and Steigner take you on a rollicking journey of revenge and retribution. ~Kim Sperduto, Esq., Award-Winning Litigator, Washington, D.C.

Fatal Accusation is a suspenseful page-turning novel. I had a hard time putting it down! I appreciate the research that was put into the medical details. A really engaging first novel—looking forward to a follow-up! ~Cheryl A. Lindstrom, MD

Fatal Accusation weaves elements of mystery, background flashbacks, and detailed descriptions that sparked my interest and curiosity. The authors ability to switch scenes was presented in a way that offered a good variety to me the reader. ~Fr. Peter O'Donnell, Parish Priest, St. John, Herington, KS

The Surgeon General should come up with a new warning for some stories, "Do not read before bedtime, you may be up longer than you planned." Stories? Or is it how well these two authors tell the story about information technology continuing to permeate and benefit our lives and about its increasing perils. Everything seems faster, everything seems amplified. Yet, the authors tell a riveting story driven by good old human emotions and desires. ~Suman Beros, Certified Digital Forensics Examiner

To my wonderful parents, Lawrence and Marguerite Riedy.
Requiescat in Pace
– M.K.R.

In loving memory of Otto and Edith Glaesel.
– T.S.

Fatal Accusation

Chapter 1

"Lawyers, lawyers. The lawyers' meeting will start in eight minutes, lawyers."

Miranda sighed. Why did the boss pick such weird times? Sometimes it was six, or fourteen. Why not a nice, round ten? Or even twenty, to give a girl time to finish a paragraph or two. She glanced at her watch: 4:10. Okay, she got it. The meeting would last just until it was time for Aaron to take the elevator down, pass the goldfish pool, exit the polished glass doors, step through the limo door opened by his chauffeur, and arrive home precisely on time for cocktail hour.

But for the meeting, Miranda might have been able to finish her brief. Unless you were in trial, or in a hospital bed with a deadly illness, however, attendance at the lawyers' meetings was not optional. Now, she would be in the office another Saturday, working on the brief.

She closed the document – oh, so close to a final first draft – and shut down the computer. A legal pad? Pen? Nah, she thought. It's Friday afternoon. Real work was not going to be on the agenda. Aaron would read a few articles aloud and spend some time on the phone. And the team would discuss tidbits about new judges, friends, and foes in the bar, and local political news.

Miranda walked out of her office just as her neighbor, Marlon, emerged from his. He was dressed in one of his Ernani suits, this one a sage and gold tweed. Tie on, if a bit loosened at the knot. Though "casual Friday" had long ago drifted across the continent from Silicon Valley and taken up residence even in the older, white-shoe law firms in the District,

Marlon's only concession to the new regime was to pad around in his socks – today a subtle green to match the suit. But, then, he had been doing that since Bill Gates was still working in his garage.

The two strolled down the corridor to Aaron's office. Just before they stepped inside Beebee, the firm's long-time administrative assistant, called out from her station behind the reception counter. "Miranda, would you take a look at this depo notice? It'll just take a sec."

"Sure," Miranda said, pausing to reach across the counter for the draft Beebee had prepared of a document announcing the date on which the witness identified therein would be made available for a formal interview, or deposition. Out of the corner of her eye, she noticed Marlon disappear into Aaron's office. "Looks fine, Beebee," Miranda said a minute later, turning to follow Marlon.

Her attention still mainly on that unfinished brief, Miranda hardly noticed the familiar venue for Aaron's frequent firm meetings. As the managing and only partner, Aaron Stein occupied the proverbial "corner office," of course. But his office was far more than just a corner. His spanned the entire floor of the firm's fourth-floor office suite. With its floor-to-ceiling windows facing downtown DC on three sides and conference table seating twenty on the opposite side of the room from Aaron's desk, a mahogany mammoth, the office spoke clearly of professional success: Clients, meetings, and money. In this, Aaron's office was of a kind with those in the big, better-known law firms in DC.

But on second look, not so much. Towering behind and to the left of Aaron's desk was a human skeleton attached to a pole embedded in a raised platform. The skeleton sported a Washington Redskins cap. Loosely around its neck hung a red, white and blue tie. The apparition seemed to be leaning on a baseball bat around which its bony fingers wrapped, tilted slightly toward Aaron. On top of the pile of magazines, articles, motions, and briefs on Aaron's desk – the usual legal paraphernalia – lay an obstetrical forceps. On the wall to Aaron's left hung a large, framed poster with "Primum non nocere" emblazoned in bold black Cyrillic script. Center stage, between the windows on the north wall, was an imposing, glossy black-and-white photo of a middle-aged black woman, life-sized, with a young man, perhaps eighteen years old, on her lap. The awkward sprawl of the tall thin man across the woman's lap and the pain etched on her face, harkened strongly to the Vatican Pieta. This mother's anguish, however, came from a lifetime of supporting her severely brain-damaged child.

Aaron's firm specialized in medical malpractice law. And his was one of, if not the best in town.

The other associates were already seated in the deep, padded maroon leather chairs arrayed in a semi-circle in front of Aaron's desk. Marlon White. Will McCarty. Cassandra Robins. Miranda Patel. Kim Heines. And the latest member of the team, Betsy Thornhill, all present except for Luke, who was on maternity leave. Miranda was proud of her crew. Few in number, it was nonetheless nicely diverse: Gay men and straight; a lesbian; Catholics, Jews, and atheists; persons of European descent and persons of color.

Also present, to Miranda's surprise, was a client. At least, she presumed it was a client. But late on a Friday afternoon? A slender woman dressed in a pink-and-white striped button-down blouse, shoulder-length blonde hair brushed and shiny, was sitting in a wheelchair parked to the far right of the semi-circle of associates' chairs, her face turned toward Aaron. The woman turned suddenly and faced the associates. Her dark blue eyes locked on Miranda, still standing behind the other, seated associates.

Oh my god, Miranda caught her breath. Her face reddened as the unstoppable wave of anger swept her. It was Jessica.

Miranda's knees shook, and she reached out a hand to steady herself on the back of Marlon's chair. Marlon craned his head around and looked hard at her, frowning. He put a finger to his lips.

"Ssshh, don't make a scene," he whispered.

"Why didn't you tell me," Miranda hissed as she twisted between Marlon's chair and her own and plopped onto the padded leather.

"I didn't know," Marlon protested.

Jessica Lane, then a bright and ambitious young woman, had worked as a paralegal for Aaron every summer while she was attending the School for Advanced International Studies at John Hopkins ("SAIS"), one of the premier graduate programs for international studies in the country. She had left the firm after graduation, almost two years ago. Bright and ambitious, Jessica was clearly on the path towards career success. But look at her now, Miranda thought, uneasily. Not in her own office working hard. Here. In a wheelchair.

Miranda glanced up. Jessica, eyes still locked on Miranda's, smiled slightly. Though the flush of anger was gone, Miranda looked away.

"Good afternoon, lawyers," Aaron interrupted Miranda's confused thoughts. He almost sounded cheerful, Miranda could not help but

3

notice. In her one-on-one meetings with Aaron, to go over the thornier legal issues in a case or discuss the expert witnesses they should target, he was stiff and brusque. Miranda knew this was true for the other associates, as well. Except for Marlon, maybe. Marlon was Aaron's first associate, the one who came on board when the firm shared an office suite with a commercial cleaning company. Aaron was almost convivial during his almost-daily meetings with the associates, however. Marlon told her Aaron was just not that comfortable with most other people unless they were assembled in a group. Like a jury.

Aaron quickly explained why they were gathered. Yesterday, Jim Kreske, one of the firm's assistants, had taken a call from Jessica. As was standard practice when someone called asking Aaron to look into a possible medical malpractice case, Jim scheduled Jessica to come in for an exploratory interview. What had happened to Jessica, in a nutshell, was that a year ago she arrived at the emergency room at Georgetown Hospital in an ambulance, unconscious. Imaging showed a massive subdural hematoma. She underwent an emergency craniotomy, which saved her life. But not the use of her limbs.

"Just tell us how you ended up in the hospital, Jessica. We'll do a full intake interview later," Aaron instructed.

"OK. Well, first, thanks so much for having me in. This has all just been so strange and difficult. So hard on my folks, emotionally, of course, but financially, too. And I ..." She stopped, voice thick. "Wasn't always sure I was going to make it."

She sighed and shifted her torso straighter in the wheelchair. "This was a year ago now. I'd just gotten a new job with McKinsey, slated to start work on an artificial intelligence consulting project for a company in the UK. Just the kind of job I'd been aiming for with my SAIS degree."

"Isn't AI all about algorithms and software? You studied international finance. What do you know about AI?" Will asked.

Aaron sighed heavily. "Will, you can find out what kind of toothpaste she uses later. Let's stick with the main story right now."

Everyone smiled. Will's depositions – detailed interviews of witnesses in a case – were famous. He believed a case could rise or fall on the tiniest detail, and if you missed it during the deposition, you were failing your client. The length of his deposition transcripts rivaled War and Peace. He drove defense counsel crazy, but he always had a legitimate argument why his questions were relevant. Everyone at the firm agreed that he was by far the best deposition taker, and Aaron inevitably had Will teach newbies the technique. But even Aaron had had to laugh the time Will asked what kind of toothpaste a defense expert witness used. Will could not remember how he had gotten that one by defense counsel. Maybe he was asleep, Marlon had suggested.

"The project wasn't about creating AI, Will," Jessica said. "It was about planning how to use it most productively."

"Anyway," she continued, "this first part of the story is short because I don't remember any of it. My neighbor in my apartment building, Sarah Hester, came home from the movies on a Friday night and noticed my door was slightly ajar. She stopped for a minute in the hallway, thinking I must be on my out, having stepped inside to grab my keys or something, or I wouldn't have left the door open. I didn't come out, though, and of course, she was worried. I've got a great building, but you sure don't leave a door unlocked in any DC neighborhood. She knocked, and when I didn't answer, she stuck her head inside. Except for the bathroom, all of my studio apartment is visible from the door. I was lying smack in the middle of the room, curled up in a fetal position. Sarah told the police she knelt, swept the hair from my face and gasped. My open eyes were all huge, black pupils. There was no 'me' in there, Sarah said in her interview. She called 911." Jessica fell silent.

"Do you remember anything at all about what happened to you?" Aaron asked.

"Nope. I don't remember anything about that day at all. Of course, who remembers a Friday from a year ago. But it's different with me. With a brain injury. I looked at my calendar for the day, and the week before, and I get what I was doing. But I can't clearly place myself anywhere or remember being with anybody. It's hard to explain. The memories are weirdly foggy and gray."

As she was talking, Jessica slowly slumped lower into her wheelchair. She bent her head and put her face in her hands momentarily. But then she straightened herself, pulling back her shoulders and smoothing her hair back behind her ears.

"What was the diagnosis from the hospital, Jessica?" Marlon asked quietly.

"I had no traumatic wounds to the head. No prior history that would explain the bleed. My blood chemistry was clean. According to the discharge summary, the cause of the hemorrhage was 'unknown.'"

"I'm not sure at this point if that's good or bad," Aaron said. "But go on. The treatment details at Georgetown and in rehab will be in your medical records. Tell us about how you are now. Are you MMI? At maximum medical improvement? And why didn't you call us before now? It's been a year, after all."

"I just got to a place where I can think about anything other than my therapy," Jessica answered his last question first. "And I just found a place to stay in DC. I don't know what I'll do, or what I can do I should say, now that I'm back. But it felt better to be here than in Houston. Back to the place where I was last normal."

Aaron nodded. "Okay. And your current status is?"

"I've recovered completely mentally, but I'm a paraplegic. Paralyzed from the waist down."

Miranda took a deep breath. Had not enough time gone by for her to get over it already? To forgive Jessica? Miranda had had these thoughts before and dismissed them. But face-to-face with Jessica in her wheelchair ... Miranda clenched her pen.

"Jessica," Marlon spoke up. "I'm a little confused here. Paraplegia is usually caused by a spinal cord injury, not an intracranial bleed. So how ..."

"Really bad luck," Jessica interrupted. "Given the size and location of my hematoma, it compressed my spinal cord. The doctors said this is extremely rare, but it can happen." She sighed. "But back to Aaron's question. Theoretically, I'm at maximum medical improvement. Cognitively, I'm back to normal. I can think as well as I ever could. Which is a miracle for which I will be eternally grateful. From my current doctors' point of view, nothing else can be done to make my body better. But I'm not done. At least I hope I'm not. I go to Georgetown for regular physical therapy, to keep my paralyzed self from deteriorating. Just last week, I met a neurology resident there who told me about a promising new treatment for neurological injuries. It's a version of stem cell therapy, but it's not yet approved by the FDA or performed here in the States. I'd have to go to the Cayman Islands for the treatment, which lasts four weeks. Hugely expensive, in other words. And definitely not covered by insurance."

Jessica paused for a moment, then continued. "I know a brain bleed can kill you. The doctors saved my life. But still. I had such terrible post-operative complications. I just wonder if something went wrong in the surgery. Or they didn't get me to surgery fast enough. I want to know what happened to me. How I got to this place. More importantly, I need the money. I need to sue. Look," she continued. "Our insurance covered a lot of the medical care I've had, but not all of it by a long shot. My parents took out a second mortgage on their home to help cover the costs. Dad cashed out his retirement account. It wasn't huge, but now it's gone. I haven't even paid off my student loans yet. We are just tapped out."

Jessica's hands tightened on the arms of her wheelchair. Then she continued, voice shaking now. "Look, I know you can't file a lawsuit unless there is a legitimate case. I'm just asking you to look into it. Because if nothing else happens, I'm in a wheelchair for the rest of my life. If I can find the funds, I have a decent chance of walking again. To have my life back. I'll be normal again."

The room was silent for a moment. Then Aaron asked: "When you say the treatment would be 'expensive,' what do you mean, Jessica? Do you have at least a rough estimate?"

"I was told I should plan on two-and-a-half million, which would include lodging and ..."

"Dollars?" Aaron interrupted her. "No, that's got to be in some different currency," he suggested

"Dollars, all right," Jessica shook her head. "You know how expensive even a routine surgery can cost if it's not covered by insurance. And this treatment is experimental but very promising. People from all over the world are trying to get into the program. Those who can afford it will pay top dollar. The rest of us have to ante up, too."

Aaron was shaking his head. "I thought maybe I," he paused. "The firm, I mean, could help out. But we just can't afford ..."

This time Jessica interrupted Aaron. "I'm not looking for charity," she said firmly. "Thanks for the kind thoughts, though," she continued, in a warmer tone. "But I just need you to work up the case. Fast."

That was an odd note, Marlon thought. Jessica knew these things took time to investigate. 'Fast' was not usually an option. "Something else, Jessica?" he asked.

"Well, there is just one more thing," Jessica said. "If this therapy is going to work, I have to start it soon. I have a window of opportunity, and when it closes, it closes for good."

Aaron scowled. "What do you mean?"

"If I don't start treatment before the end of this year, I will never get any better. I'll be a paraplegic for the rest of my life."

One Week Earlier

Chad glanced at his watch and drained his glass of wine. Fittingly enough, the player piano in the first-class lounge of Istanbul Ataturk

Airport was playing New York, New York. Not quite it, but close. Chad was flying Turkish Air back to D.C. He had thought a face-to-face meeting unnecessary at this point. Risky for him, too, given the state of play. But his presence had been demanded, so he had to make the trip. He would make sure to keep a low profile. Fly in, do what he had to do, and fly out.

He had plenty of time before boarding. He went back to the closest bar, asked for another glass of wine, and returned to his table where he had left his bag. He sipped his wine appreciatively.

A short time later Chad sat comfortably in his first-class cocoon. Baggage stored in the roomy, overhead compartment. Shoes off, slippers from the "comfort kit" given him by the solicitous attendant on, seat reclined, flute of champagne on the spacious armrest of his equally capacious, padded leather seat. A long but pleasant flight ahead. He would have plenty of time to think.

Chapter 2

1985

Fort Riley lay in a valley between Manhattan, Kansas (the "Little Apple" as the locals called it) and Junction City, bordered by Interstate 70 on the south. Passersby blasting through the "fly-over states" at eighty-five miles per hour, rounding the long curves of the highway as it traversed the Flint Hills, caught a glimpse of rows of Quonset huts on gray macadam, jeeps parked neatly outside, a few gigantic, warehouse-type buildings, and an airport runway. Only a few retirees, with time on their hands, would enter the Fort through the visitor's entrance on the east side to tour the Custer and U.S. Cavalry museums.

Ft. Riley was the home of the "Big Red One," the First Infantry Division of the U.S. Army and the oldest continuously serving unit, having fought in W.W. I. A long list of well-known Americans had been stationed at Ft. Riley over the years, including George Custer, Jackie Robinson, and Dwight Eisenhower.

Beyond the perimeter visible from the highway lay a sprawling community, covering one hundred sixty square miles, complete with office complexes, housing, schools, and a couple of swimming pools in addition to parade grounds and training fields. Roughly twenty-five thousand enlisted men and women and civilians worked on the base, and it was a significant component of the economy of the surrounding region, second only to Kansas State University in Manhattan. Except for the rare foray into Junction City with his mother to shop for some item not available in the commissary, this was Chad Blakely's world.

On a warm, sunny day in October, Chad was almost out the front door when he stopped, turned, and yelled back into the house: "I'm going over to Ed's," he called. His mother's curly-haired head appeared around the kitchen door frame. "Okay, honey, but back no later than 9:00." Chad gave a little wave and took off.

Thirteen years old, Chad had changed little since he entered kindergarten. Just over four feet, he was the shortest boy in his class. Most of the others' voices had broken, and his male classmates had gotten visibly taller and broader across the shoulders. Not Chad. Instead, he knew, with his slender frame, round brown eyes framed with long, thick lashes, and silky blonde hair, worn longer than was fashionable because it was the way his mother liked it, he still looked girlish. His classmates teased him about it, yelling "wrong one" when he pushed the door labeled "Boys," and pushing him out of the boys' line when the teacher lined them up to go out for recess.

Chad tried not to care. It was just words, after all, and he had been told many times that "words will never hurt you." He had not had to contend with any roughing up. Discipline was strict all over the base, for one thing, and unless it was in a controlled environment like a boxing ring, the boys were rarely at liberty to beat up on each other. Anyway, he thought he could hold his own if anything happened. He did not look it, maybe, but he was strong for his age. He ran up and down on the trails in hills surrounding the Fort, bounded by thick, tall prairie grass, looking for fossilized shark teeth or coyote scat. He biked all over the base and threw baseballs at the bull's eye he had drawn in chalk on the garage door.

Besides, it was always going to be something. Army couples, moving from station to station around the country and across the globe, formed self-sufficient units. Siblings were a close-knit team. They fought like cats and dogs among themselves, but they stuck by each other against outsiders. Kids made friends from other families, of course, but it took effort, and true allegiance always remained with the family. For most kids Chad knew, these facts were no big deal. The family tribe was big enough. Military couples, like others during that era, tended to have large families. Chad, however, was an only child. Well, practically an only child. He was an easy target.

But now he had Ed. Ed was one of the new kids in Chad's eighth-grade class. A batch of new kids started every semester. The teachers had long ago instituted a student mentoring system, pairing newcomers with those who had been around at least a year. The young mentors explained what really happened during home-room; which textbooks needed to be hauled around, and which could be left in lockers; whom to avoid during recess; and all those other survival techniques that the teachers either did not really know or did not want to take the time to try to explain. Chad was paired with Ed.

When they first sat down together after the first day of class, Chad feigned indifference. It was the safer course. Other semesters he had tried to get chummy with his assigned buddy. But it had never worked out, and the rejection stung. Chad had learned to pay little heed to his so-called buddy. But Ed wouldn't have it. Instead, Ed enthused about what a great idea it was to pair the kids, and how he was happy Chad was to be his new buddy, then launched into a series of questions about Chad and his family and where all they had. Only the teachers ever asked. Chad was initially dubious. Ed was evidently brownnosing for some as-yet-unknown reason. But when Ed explained that he was also an only child, Chad got it. Ed was for real. And so it began.

It took some time before the two boys figured out how to contour their friendship, however. Both were loners. Chad loved running in the hills; Ed preferred laps in the pool. Chad was good at math; Ed loathed algebra and loved to read, and their speech class. He was the only eighth-grader who volunteered to read an epic poem or an oration in front of the class. The two also had entirely different relationships at home.

Chad loved his parents, he supposed, but he rarely spent time with them except during of meals. Chad's father, Tom Blakely, who had been on the verge of adulthood at the time the nation learned of the heroic exploits of the Manhattan Project, dreamed of becoming a physicist. He was accepted at Cal Tech and showed some early promise. But he suffered a nervous collapse in his senior year of college, almost a year after he had met the woman who would become Chad's mother. They married when Chad's father had sufficiently recovered, and shortly thereafter, his father joined the Army, beginning a long career in logistics. Chad had only a foggy idea about all this. All he knew for sure was that his father was quiet and distant. He read a lot and left Chad largely to his own devices. His mother, Amy, was a mother like any other, Chad supposed.

Ed's father, on the other hand, loomed large in his son's life. Ed was always relating to Chad things he had done with his dad. He had taken Ed into the hills and taught him to hunt. Ed and his dad regularly went fishing, weather permitting, in nearby Milford Lake. His dad had long ago bought Ed a tool kit and showed him how to use them all. They talked about everything, Ed told Chad, "even sex." Chad was shocked at that.

The first time Chad met this paragon was when Ed invited him over to sit in on one of his dad's "life lessons." Ed did not at first explain what this was, and Chad was hesitant. A lecture from a male adult, not a teacher sounded peculiar and decidedly not fun to Chad. But Ed was clearly eager, and assured Chad that he would like his dad who was "really a great guy." Chad went, given the promise of dinner afterward, and with the dim notion that this would be a good way to cement his friendship with Ed.

Chad knocked on Ed's family's door at 6:30, as instructed. The door was opened by a tall, burly man, dark-haired, with startlingly blue eyes, like his son, dressed in the ubiquitous khaki. He reached out a beefy, gnarly hand and grabbed Chad's, shaking it firmly. "Chad," he intoned in a loud, bass voice. "Sergeant Dante. Call me Sarge. Nice to meet you. Come on in and be sure to wipe your feet."

Chad hesitated a moment. But catching a glimpse of Ed coming up behind his father, wide grin on his face, he carefully wiped his feet on the mat in front of the door and walked in. Ed's home, also in the non-commissioned officer's housing on the base, had the same floor plan as Chad's. Chad walked into the living room, left front; seeing the smaller bedroom, left-right, through the door off the living room. He followed Ed into the smallish, eat-in kitchen, left-rear; to the right of which was undoubtedly the master bedroom. Ed introduced his mother, Clara, who welcomed Chad from her station in front of the stove, stirring something steaming in a large pot. Chad was only thirteen, but even he realized that Clara was a very attractive woman. Ed then motioned Chad back out to the living room where his father had taken a seat on an orange-ish and tan patterned sofa. The boys sat cross-legged on the beige shag carpet in front of the sofa.

"Let me tell you a story," Ed's father began. His voice was still loud, but warmer, somehow, Chad thought. Inviting. Like that one missionary from India who'd been visiting his childhood home in Kansas and came to preach at their church last summer. Chad looked over at Ed. Ed was sitting up straight, shoulders back, eyes glued to his father. He glanced at Chad. Ed's eyes shone, and he had a pleased look on his face. This was a gift, Chad realized. Ed sharing his father with Chad.

On an unseasonably warm day in late November, Chad and Ed sat on the baseball field, backs to the chain-link fence behind home base. School was done for the day, and the two had a few minutes before they were both due home for chores. They were discussing Sarge's latest "life lesson" from the previous Saturday evening. Ed's father was a devout Methodist, read the Bible regularly and, emulating what he thought of as a brilliant as well as God-given method of imparting indelible lessons, used parables to teach his son, now joined by Chad, how an upright, American man should live. Sarge would tell a story. The boys were to go away and ponder it and return with their take on the embedded lesson. Sarge would correct and clarify as necessary.

Sarge had enlisted in 1944 and served the remainder of the War, though to his lifelong regret he was never sent Overseas, spending his time, instead, working on a construction crew erecting barracks in Fort Cronkhite in the Marin headlands in California under the command of the Quartermaster General. He had then chosen a career as an Army man. It followed, then, that his parables were often based on something he had observed or learned in the Army, or on some event from military history.

The boys had studied American history and, from military families, naturally knew quite a bit about the World Wars. They knew about the Armistice, signed on the eleventh hour of the eleventh day of the eleventh month, in 1918, knew France had fallen to the Germans in 1941 and knew that Hitler had committed suicide in his bunker in Berlin in April of 1945. But Ed's father filled in a few more details Saturday night.

"The Armistice was signed in a railroad car in the Compiegne Forest in France. Just over twenty years later, Hitler made Petain return to that car to surrender France to the Nazis. This, to the Germans, symbolized the utter humiliation of the French, payback for what France and its allies had done to Germany after W.W. I: Treated Germany not as a worthy foe, defeated only after an honorable and costly fight, but as a vassal state, forced to pay reparations and cede German territory, and excluded from any role as the victorious nations re-drew the map of the world, dividing up the pre-war empires into sovereign nations. Four years later, after the deaths of tens of millions of people and the destruction of Europe, Hitler was dead, and the Nazis defeated."

Ed's father had paused, then looked sternly at the boys. "W.W. I was supposed to be the War to End All Wars. That didn't happen, obviously, for lots of complicated reasons. But what's the lesson for you boys, here?

You triumph over somebody: You're France. What should you do differently?" Then he shooed them away.

"I think I've got it," Ed said as he flopped over onto his stomach, soaking up the warmth of the black macadam court. "Have you heard of Machiavelli?" he asked his friend.

"Nope. Not a clue," Chad responded lazily.

"I've been trying to read his book, 'The Prince.'" Ed said. "By Machiavelli, who was a sort of tutor, I think, to an Italian prince. Machiavelli came up with rules for how to be a powerful prince. Or king, or president, I guess. Whatever. And wrote a book about it. Mr. Hoffman said it's really famous and people still think Machiavelli's rules make sense even though he wrote them hundreds of years ago."

"So, I'm guessing you think your dad's story was about one of those rules?" Chad asked.

"Yep. Here it is. If you strike an enemy, you have to hit him hard enough that he can't ever come back and get you. 'Cause he will if you don't," Joe said firmly.

Chad thought for a minute, then asked: "Does your dad know about this Machiavelli, do you suppose?"

Ed shrugged. "Don't know. But I got the feeling from Mr. Hoffman that lots of people know about his rules even if they've never heard of Machiavelli. Anyway," he continued, "sure seems to be the right lesson from that story."

It was Chad's turn to shrug. "Maybe. Or maybe it's about not kicking someone when they're down. Or not kicking so hard, anyway. Remember, Sarge said Germany was a 'worthy foe,' whatever that means. I don't know ..." he trailed off, frowning.

Ed just laughed. "I don't really know, either. Oh, well, Dad will straighten it out. Come on, time to get going." Chad stood, extending a hand to Ed, who grabbed it and pulled himself up, and the boys walked home.

The next morning, Chad's mother had just served pancakes when the phone rang. The phone hung on the living room wall right around the corner from the kitchen door, so Chad and his father could clearly hear her side of the conversation. "Hello? Oh, good morning, Martha." She paused, listening. "Oh, that's just terrible," his mother's voice rose. She tutted. "That poor family. We didn't know him at all well, but Chad's good friends with the boy. Ed."

"What is it?" Chad asked.

His mother turned to Chad and mouthed, "just a minute," holding up her index finger.

"I suppose it's too soon for arrangements to have been made. Do let me know if you hear anything," his mother continued. "I'll run a casserole over because we know the boy, but I don't want to bother her asking questions." Pause. "Okay, I'll talk to you later, Martha." She hung up, came into the kitchen, and sat. "Terrible news, I'm afraid. Ed's father died last night. Dropped dead from a heart attack, apparently."

Chad felt an unfamiliar knot gathering in his stomach. For a minute, he thought he was going to be sick. That passed, but he still felt unsettled. Distant from his body, somehow.

"You'll stay home from school this morning, Chad. I'll call the principal's office. I'll whip up a casserole, and then we'll go over to see Ed and Clara. A widow now. Just can't imagine." She shook her head.

Chad could not imagine it, either. He had never been in a house where someone has just died. He did not know any other kid who had lost a parent. The only death he had had any contact with had been at his grandfather's funeral in Cleveland when Chad was ten. His grandfather had been an old man and his mother, who had lost her father, was sad during the service, but she laughed with her sisters at the reception afterward. He did not know what it would be like at Ed's house right now, but he was quite sure he did not want to know.

"I don't want to go," Chad choked out past the growing lump in his throat.

"Don't be ridiculous," his mother said firmly as she rose from the table, the pancakes on her plate untouched. She opened the refrigerator and started pulling out ingredients for her casserole. "He's your best friend. Don't be such a child."

Chad looked at his father. "Dad, do I have to?"

His father shrugged. "Just do as your mother says."

An hour later, Chad sat uneasily next to Ed. He had crept into the room when Ed's mother opened the door and pointed inside. Ed was sitting on the edge of his bed, back stooped, shoulders hunched, and his head seemed to have sunk into his neck. He had clearly been crying, and from his pinched face and rubbery limbs, Chad could tell Ed had not gotten much sleep if any. Ed had not said a word or even looked at Chad. Chad had no idea what to say or do. Then he felt Ed tremble. Chad turned, put his arm around Ed's shoulders and hugged.

Chapter 3

The following Monday, promptly at 10:00, Jessica was back in the office, as instructed. The lawyers were meeting to discuss what to do about her case. Jessica was to be available in the event they had any questions for her. Marlon met her at the reception desk, thanked her for coming, and wheeled her into the small conference room just off the main door to the office suite. Jim, who was to keep Jessica company, was already present and greeted her warmly. Marlon headed for Aaron's office.

Jim did not have an official title, but he could be called the "client handler." He scheduled client meetings with the lawyers; called clients to remind them to bring in documents; and screened client calls. Most times, the client had nothing to say about the case itself but just wanted to talk. Jim chatted with the clients and saved the lawyers' time. He knew the clients' spouses and the names of their children, and generally, what had brought them to Aaron. But he did not know and usually did not care to know about the medical details. But this was Jessica. This time he wanted to know.

"So, unless you don't want to talk about it, what actually happened to you?" Jim asked as he pulled a chair back from the table, cocked it to face the wheelchair, and sat.

"No, I'm okay talking about it, Jim," Jessica replied. "I had a hematoma inside my skull," she continued. "Which means bleeding inside my head. A hematoma is often, though not always caused by trauma. If you kick a concrete wall and smash your toe, the trauma will cause internal bleeding. You see the bleed as a bruise. In most parts of the body, the bleeding is distributed to surrounding tissue, so you will get some swelling from the bleed at the point of the trauma but not a lot. A subdural hematoma is a bleed inside the dura, a thick, protective covering around the brain. The dura doesn't expand very much, so as the bleeding continues, the brain is compressed against the skull. The surgeons had to drill a hole in my skull, stop the bleeding, and suction out the pool of blood that had collected. The sequelae ..."

"The what?" Jim interrupted. "You sound just like a doctor, I swear."

Jessica smiled. "I've had a lot of time to read up on it," she explained. "And ask questions of everyone along the way."

Jim nodded. That sounded like the Jessica he had worked with, all right.

"Anyway, the consequences, in other words," Jessica continued. "My brain was severely damaged when it was compressed inside the dura. You have a general idea, I presume, what causes a concussion: a hard hit to the head, which makes your brain rattle around inside your skull. Anyway, with a concussion, you get dizzy and nauseous and can have some short-term memory and concentration problems. Well, imagine not just a brief rattle, but a prolonged flattening."

"How awful! Poor girl," Jim said, shaking his head.

"When I woke from surgery, I was helpless," Jessica resumed. "I was like a baby again. I couldn't eat. I wore a diaper. I couldn't talk and couldn't even remember any words. My first memory is about three months after the surgery. I suddenly realized that the woman who was sleeping in a chair beside my hospital-style bed was my mother."

"God, I wish I could forget who my mother was for a couple of months," Jim blurted. At the look on Jessica's face, Jim apologized. "I know, I know, sorry. But if you knew my mother ... Okay, back to it."

"It took months of intensive therapy before I could formulate a word," Jessica continued. "I woke up in the morning, looked around, and said, 'Mom.' Mom burst into tears, knowing it would upset me but unable to stop. But I don't remember much about that time. It was the next six months that were so hard. I had to re-learn to use my muscles. Let's just say it hurt. A lot."

"And that's just the physical therapy," Jessica continued. "I remember trying to repeat the damn alphabet, and I kept leaving out p-q-r-s over and over, and I can't begin to tell you how frustrated and angry and furious and terribly sad that made me because some part of my brain was appalled at how stupid I had become. I would still be playing with big wooden blocks except for my mother and the saints at St. Andrew's, who got me through that stage."

"After that, I moved back to Houston for my second in-patient rehab. My being in Houston was a lot easier on my parents, of course."

Jim nodded. He knew Houston was Jessica's home town.

"That's where I learned how to live with my paraplegia," Jessica continued. "And get over my depression. You know, people in wheelchairs can be just as happy as anyone else. But it takes an awful lot of work to get there."

"But wait a minute," Jim said, "let's go back to the beginning. What caused the bleed? What sent you to the hospital in the first place?"

"I have no idea," Jessica said flatly. "The only thing I know is that my neighbor found me unconscious. She had nothing to do with what happened to me, though. Police checked that out. She's clean as a whistle."

Jim shook his head. They fell silent.

While Jessica was relaying her story to Jim, the assembled lawyers discussed her case.

"I don't like it," Aaron concluded. "Something bad obviously happened to her before the neighbor called the ambulance. Maybe an accident, or maybe something criminal. Anyway, we don't know. The police came up empty, and Jessica has no memory of what happened. So, it seems to me that what caused the bleed originally will remain a mystery. Even if our experts do identify some negligence in her treatment at the hospital or in the ambulance, the jury would likely blame the mysterious original head injury for her damages, not the EMT or the doctors."

"Aaron," Marlon said firmly. "She's one of us. We should at least give it a try."

Aaron sighed. He tipped his chair back, lacing his hands behind his head, staring over the heads of his row of his associates at the bustling canyon of Connecticut Avenue stretching north from the office. The newest firm picture hanging on the wall across the room caught his eye. In this one, the lawyers were gathered at the foot of the Washington Monument. The sky behind the Monument was bright blue, and every flag on the poles circling its base stood briskly at attention, pointing north. His new public relations coordinator, Caroline Haines, had done a nice job, he thought.

The associates sat silently, all eyes on Aaron. After a few long minutes, he sighed again. "But it's impossible," he grumped. "We don't have enough time. Jessica has, what, about four months before she'd have to start the treatment? The usual med mal case from getting the medical records to jury verdict or settlement takes two years."

"I think we can do it," Marlon objected. "If there's a case," he continued. "For one thing, Georgetown has a new, digital medical record system and is promising an expedited response to a request. We can send Jessica over to get her own records, which will make it even quicker."

Will jumped in. "Dr. Franklin is a top-notch neurosurgeon, and he would agree to review the records quickly and give us his opinion on whether there was malpractice in the surgical procedure, or not."

"And Aaron, remember we got the Heiman settlement offer a week after sending over the draft complaint, it was such a clear case of negligence," Marlon said, standing as he spoke. "We'll know in a week or so if we have a Heiman-variety case. I can draft the complaint in an hour if we do. We'll try for a quick settlement. If we don't have a case, we've still done all we can to help."

Aaron nodded. After all, if there was malpractice, it was a high-profile and lucrative case. "Okay, let's get started. We'll get the medical records and have them reviewed. STAT."

The lawyers drifted out of Aaron's office, discussing the "to-dos" on Jessica's case. "Miranda, you've got the freest calendar right now, so why don't you take the lead," Marlon said.

"But I've got a trial coming up," Miranda objected.

"What are you talking about?" Marlon frowned. "That's months away." He waved at Miranda dismissively as he turned and started down the corridor. "Grow up, Miranda."

Back in her office, Miranda stood behind her desk, looking out the window. Just do it, she told herself. Start with the trial calendar.

For every new case, the firm created a trial calendar, with actions to be taken on specified dates. Once a trial date was set for a case, that date would become the "final deadline." The number of days remaining before trial would be entered on a "trial clock." Any lawyer having cases with trial dates pending kept close track of the trial clock. So much had to be done to be ready for trial that every day counted. You just could not fall behind. It used to be the job of an assistant to change the trial clocks daily for all active cases, an onerous task. These days it was done electronically.

At least once a month the firm had a must-attend, Saturday morning meeting to check the calendar of every case in the office. At this calendar call, completed actions would be checked off the list and new ones added, and due dates adjusted if the work just had not gotten done yet or the court had issued a revised case scheduling order. Aaron used the calendar call to make sure all the firm's cases were moving promptly through the pipeline, from intake to trial or settlement. But the main objective of the exercise was to avoid missing a critical deadline.

The final deadline for new cases, which did not yet have a trial date, was the day the statute of limitations would run. By law, a plaintiff must file a lawsuit within the time set by this statute. For Aaron's cases, almost all claiming negligence, a plaintiff usually had three years, beginning from the date the negligence occurred. One day late and the case was time-barred. Thrown out of court. Aaron would get sued for malpractice. To avoid that calamitous event, the lawyers checked and re-checked the date entered on the trial calendar for when the statute would run.

Miranda calculated the statute of limitations – a little less than two years out – and entered it on Jessica's trial calendar, making a note to confirm the date was accurate when she had had the medical records in hand. As instructed by Aaron, she entered the Final Deadline much sooner. Trial Clock: 30.

A few minutes later Miranda, as usual, was running late for her Monday night regular, drinks with Kay. She should walk briskly up the escalator from the Dupont Circle metro station, to make up some time. The exercise would not hurt, either, particularly since she had once again skipped the gym. She looked up at the far-away oval exit framing the dusky sky, shuddered, and stayed put on the right-hand railing. Let the machine do the work.

Emerging onto Q Street, Miranda headed north to Le Tomate, one of the many restaurant bars in one of the city's favorite night spots. It was, of course, hot and sultry, this being August in Washington, and a massive bank of purplish cumulus clouds rose above the sun low in the west. It would probably be raining cats and dogs when they left the bar later. Rather than engage in the battle of the umbrellas getting back down to the metro on the crowded sidewalks, Miranda would get Kay to drive her home.

Not for the first time, Miranda pondered the different career paths she and Kay were on. Kay, a hot-shot lawyer at the State Department, a position coveted for its prestige and international glamour. Though Miranda was proud of the work she did, she knew med mal lawyers were popularly scorned as "ambulance chasers" and privately, if not publicly deemed second-class citizens by attorneys with other specialties. But the loudest critics came to Aaron pleading for help when their wife/father/daughter had a bad outcome in an encounter with the health care system. And those whom Aaron and his associates successfully represented – and they almost always won – remained lifelong friends and supporters. The med mal defense bar also respected Aaron and the other members of his firm for their consistent professionalism, extensive preparation, and courtesy, even in the heat of a litigation battle.

Her day-to-day work was satisfying, too. Her clients were, for the most part, nice, hard-working people who had experienced some variety of medical catastrophe that bereaved them, dramatically changed their lives, and left them with large, unpaid medical bills. The firm could not actually fix these things, but at least they might ease the financial pain. The legal work was challenging, particularly the trials. Four-ring circuses, she always thought, requiring total concentration on the judge, the jury, the witness, and opposing counsel. And she was among the select few with actual trials under her belt because these days lawyers rarely tried cases unless they were in the med mal or criminal bar.

Approaching the wide plate-glass windows of Le Tomate, Miranda saw that Kay had, thankfully, managed to snag a high-top in the corner of the bar area, and, yes! Already had two glasses of wine. Miranda walked in, leaned over and gave Kay a peck on the cheek as she sat. "Thank you, thank you, and you won't believe who came into the office last Friday."

"Well, tell," Kay said wryly. "Who?"

"Jessica," Miranda said, voice strained.

"Oh, no," Kay said, voice flat.

Miranda had told Kay all about Jessica, of course. For whatever reason, from literally Jessica's first day at the firm, she and Miranda had bonded. Miranda and Jessica liked the same restaurants and disliked the gym, though both vowed to go more often. Both enjoyed a good bottle of wine and preferred the symphony to jazz. They did things together, but neither felt the need for exclusivity, and Jessica became friendly with many of Miranda's friends, and vice-versa. Jessica became a regular at Miranda's weekly dinners with her mom.

And as these things sometimes go, Miranda got lucky in another department at about the same time. She had not had a serious boyfriend in five years, despite her sustained efforts on Match.com and regular introductions to possible mates among friends-of-friends. But then along came Patrick Connolly, who was defending his witness at a deposition taken by Miranda. Bright, energetic, witty, handsome, red-haired Patrick. Miranda was smitten, and at first, the feeling seemed mutual.

But then Patrick met Jessica at a Bar function. He fell hard. And wooed her hard, too. Of course, Miranda thought. The younger blonde.

At first, Jessica refused to go out with Patrick and told Miranda so. Miranda told her to go ahead, though. It was all over for Miranda, anyway. Patrick had no interest in her anymore.

Miranda hoped and expected that Jessica would stay loyal, though. When Jessica started dating Patrick, Miranda hurt. A lot.

Very soon Patrick's interest in Jessica waned, too. But it was too late. For Miranda, anyway. Jessica argued that it was not her fault, and if it had not been Jessica, it would have been someone else who came between Miranda and Patrick. Patrick was just not a man to commit. Probably never would. Their friendship was strong enough to weather this storm, Jessica pleaded.

Miranda walked away from it, though. She was acting just like her mother, Miranda had thought. For better or worse. Anyway, Miranda could not let go of her anger and hurt.

Then her mom, Paula, got sick. Pancreatic cancer. It was shocking and sudden. Three months from the diagnosis and her mother was dead. Between the doctors' appointments and the chemo and the hospitalizations and trying to stay cheerful for each other, and then arranging for hospice care, Miranda and her mother had time for little but dealing with dying.

Clearly, near the end – her mother was conscious, but barely, her breathing slow and shallow, cheeks drawn, eye sockets sunken – on that Friday morning, her step-father, Bill, left Miranda alone with her mother. Miranda eyes filled with tears as she stroked her mother's thin hand.

Suddenly, her mom started breathing heavily, chest heaving. She struggled to draw air through the fluid that was filling her chest and lungs. Miranda shuddered at the horrible, deep gurgle she had been told about by the hospice nurse. Miranda stood, opened the door and called: "Bill, come in. It's the death rattle." Turning back to the bed, Miranda watched her mother's labored breathing. Her hands lay crossed and still, however.

Thank god the morphine was working, Miranda thought. A few minutes later, her mother died.

At the funeral, Aaron told her to take a week off. Miranda wasn't sure it was the greatest idea. At least at work, she would have something else about which to think. But she did. She was not up to planning a big trip, though, so she just arranged to stay at her friend Sully's little cabin out near Middleburg. Spring was in full bloom, and it was a beautiful place to hide out, read, and take long walks through the woods.

When she left the cabin after that week, Miranda thought she had gotten some things sorted out. But the first time she encountered Jessica in the office, she felt sick. Miranda avoided Jessica as much as possible after that. She made up a reason she had to skip Jessica's graduation from SAIS though everyone else at the firm, attorneys and staff, attended. Marlon frowned at her disbelievingly when Miranda explained why she could not go. He did not say anything, though.

Miranda came to realize that she had confounded her feelings about Jessica with the pain and sorrow of her mother's death. She knew this was crazy and tried to talk herself out of it. But it was all just too tiring, so she stopped thinking about it. Months went by, and there wasn't any reason to think about it. She thought.

"But then there she was, in a wheelchair," Miranda told Kay, explaining what had happened. "And I'm in charge of investigating her case," Miranda continued.

"I can imagine how you feel about that," Kay said wryly.

Miranda shrugged. "I'll do my job," she said. "Let's talk about something else," she commanded. Reaching over to raise her wine glass, Miranda took a large swig. "Glass empty," she observed. "Yours, too. I'll get us re-fills. Hang on; I'll be right back."

After placing her order at the crowded bar, Miranda glanced at the man on the bar-stool beside her. She barely had time to notice a decent looking guy, a little older, with longish blonde hair when the phone in her purse rang. She grabbed inside, fumbled with the phone, and dropped it. The device skittered on the floor and disappeared under the seated legs of the blonde guy beside her. He promptly hopped off his stool, bent over and retrieved the phone. It took a couple of minutes to extract it from the thicket of chair legs and feet and whatever else was down there, Miranda supposed.

As he was handing it back to her, he tapped the screen a few times. "Seems fine," he said.

Miranda began her thanks just as the drinks came and the man on her other side reached for something and knocked one of them over, spilling wine over the bar and onto Miranda's lap. Miranda jumped up, brushing wine off her pants, the man apologized, the waitress brought over napkins, and when the dust settled the blonde guy was gone.

Chapter 4

Wednesday, just after 2:00, Miranda stepped out of the office building and quickly ran through her options. Dr. Franklin's office on George Washington Circle was only a few blocks away. It would be a hot and steamy walk, though. September was right around the corner, but there was still no relief from the summer heat. On the other hand, she would be competing with the thousands of other lawyers and lobbyists and tourists moving around downtown Washington in the early afternoon, trying to hail a cab or summon an Uber. She would walk. She would be a little sweaty when she got there, but she would be on time. She hustled west on I Street.

At exactly 2:15, Miranda gave her name to the receptionist. A nurse escorted her down a corridor and into the doctor's office. From behind the desk, he stood, smiled, and reached out to shake Miranda's hand. "It's nice to meet you," he said. "I've reviewed Jessica's chart, so any questions you have I'm prepared to answer. Please go ahead."

Miranda was pleasantly surprised. Most of the surgeons she had met on the job were arrogant and impatient. This guy was actually nice. Attractive, too: taller than Miranda at maybe five-ten, slender, coffee au lait complexion, dark brown eyes, and close-cropped, salt-and-pepper hair. He had good taste in office décor, too. Two large maps of the world, antiques it appeared, given the strange contours of the continents depicted, beautifully framed, hung side-by-side on the sage-colored walls, the color of which was echoed in the pattern of the Persian rug. A deep cherry desk, empty except for a gorgeous, purple and yellow orchid in a crystal vase, dark maroon leather chairs, and deep, built-in bookshelves filled with leather-bound books. Miranda wondered, very briefly, if Dr. Franklin might be single; he wore no ring. She quickly pushed the thought out of her head to get down to business.

Jim and Jessica had gone to Georgetown and ordered her medical records early Tuesday morning. Jessica returned to pick them up that afternoon. Such a turn-around would have been impossible if she had requested her entire file, which was mountainous. She had been in the hospital three weeks after her surgery. It had taken that long to stabilize her enough to transfer to rehab. But the lawyers figured that if there was any malpractice, it would have been immediately before, or during the surgery. Maybe the early hours in intensive care. To expedite getting the documents, they had instructed Jessica to request only the records for her first twenty-four hours of care at the hospital and the notes from the ambulance transport, a copy of which would be in her Georgetown file. They would get the entire file later if they had a case.

Tuesday evening Jim hand-delivered the records to Dr. Franklin's home in Bethesda. Dr. Franklin, the expert who would review the case and provide the firm with his opinion as to whether any surgical malpractice had been committed, had promised he would be ready with his evaluation the next day. He was doing the firm a real favor, certainly. He was also going to charge a small fortune. But it would be worth it, given the tight time frame within which they were working. The lawyers knew, based on experience, that given a major surgical repair such as Jessica had had, the most likely candidate for any medical negligence in the care was the surgery. They would have other experts look at the chart, too. But having this early evaluation from their neurosurgical expert would give them a very good idea whether they would have a case or not.

Once Miranda was settled, Dr. Franklin quickly got down to business. He walked Miranda through his notes and the surgical report from Jessica's surgery, then assured Miranda that in his opinion, the Georgetown surgeon had provided only excellent care. The other providers, including the EMTs and the radiologists who reviewed Jessica's initial scans, were outside the area of his expertise, of course.

Miranda then turned to her question about causation. On what may have sent Jessica to the hospital in the first place. In the end, it might not be terribly important. If the nurses in the neurological intensive care unit had failed properly to monitor Jessica's intracranial pressure post-op, for example, it might not matter what started Jessica's bleed in the first place.

But best to cover all bases. Miranda surprised herself by feeling torn. The whole situation stirred unsettling emotions she thought she had put behind her. But at the same time, something else she could not quite get a handle on yet was brewing in her thinking about this case.

Miranda read aloud from the discharge summary: "'Unknown etiology, presumed trauma.' So they don't know what caused the bleed, but the best guess is trauma?" she asked.

"Well, I wouldn't call it a guess," Dr. Franklin objected. "A hemorrhage results when an artery or a vein ruptures. A rupture can be caused by a sudden increase in arterial pressure against aged or cholesterol-damaged vessels, as in a stroke, or by a scalpel during an intracranial surgical procedure. Jessica was a young woman, and she did not have hypercholesterolemia. She had not had a recent surgery. That leaves as the most likely cause an external force or trauma."

"Jessica's hemorrhage was massive, wasn't it?" Miranda objected. "She almost died. Wouldn't that mean she had to have had a really powerful blow to the head? But according to the records, she didn't even have a bruise on her skull, right? No blood, no abrasion. I'm not getting it," Miranda admitted.

"Your confusion is understandable," Dr. Franklin responded, kindly. "But every person is built a little differently. Some people's symptoms of a disease will be alleviated by a drug while others won't be affected at all, by that same drug. Everything is on a spectrum. On either end of that spectrum are the outliers. Regarding brain trauma, on one end of the spectrum is somebody with a very hard head. On the other is what you lawyers call the 'eggshell plaintiff.' A person who suffers great injury from a cause that wouldn't even bother most people."

Miranda, surprised, asked: "How in the world do you know the term eggshell plaintiff? I thought it was only used in tort class in law school."

Dr. Franklin, momentarily, looked pained. "Let's just say I had such a patient once, a long time ago. My lawyer explained it all to me in the course of the lawsuit."

"Oh, sorry," Miranda mumbled. She shouldn't have brought up the topic or the memory. She was in the business of suing doctors. And she believed in what she was doing. But she had a great deal of respect for the medical profession. She did her work not to punish or humiliate doctors, but only to help her clients when they had legitimate cause to complain about the care they had been given.

"Anyway," Dr. Franklin continued, "by way of example, a case was reported in the medical literature in which a woman rode a roller coaster, and a week later she was in the hospital with a substantial subdural hematoma. Thousands of other people safely rode that same roller coaster. Jessica may have been another such outlier. Minor trauma, major bleed."

"Okay," Miranda sighed. "So, Jessica might have bumped her head on her refrigerator door and ended up in a wheelchair. Truly a scary thought. What a fragile thing the human body is." The image of her mother's dying face flitted through her mind. Miranda shook her head. Focus, she told herself.

"Any other possible causes, Doctor?" she asked.

"Surely," replied Dr. Franklin. "Several pharmacological agents can cause intracranial hemorrhage. Belladonna, a weapon in the arsenal of assassins for centuries, is one, and other drugs in the belladonna family."

"If she was drugged," Miranda interrupted, sensing a long if learned description of that chemical family coming, "wouldn't that have shown up in the blood screen?"

"Probably not," said the doctor. "A comprehensive blood screen requires a considerable amount of time. They wouldn't have had that kind of time given the shape Jessica was in when she got to the ER. Besides, one orders a complete screen only if it is necessary for diagnosis or treatment, and that wasn't needed for Jessica. CT showed the bleed, and the necessary surgical intervention was obvious: Drill a hole in the skull to relieve the pressure. The blood work done on Jessica only screened for those drugs that regularly send people to the ER: heroin, crack cocaine, LSD. Negative for those. A truly massive amount of an unusual drug, like belladonna, might also have been detected. Negative for that. A dosage sufficient to cause a bleed in a person with a special susceptibility to the drug would fly under the radar."

Hmm. All interesting enough, Miranda thought. But it did not seem at all likely that anyone would have wanted to poison Jessica.

After her thanks and a suggestion that she might contact Dr. Franklin again after consulting with her colleagues, Miranda took her leave. She headed back to L Street for her next meeting of the day, on another case. As she walked, she called Marlon at the office, de-briefed him, and asked whether she was expected back at the office later. Marlon told her no. Will was meeting with Jessica and would report in the morning. Miranda ended the call. Crap, she had forgotten to call Jessica. To let her know they had decided to investigate the case. Conveniently forgot, she supposed. Just like that time when she had conveniently forgotten to take her cousin to that dance.

Miranda had been a sophomore in high school. She was supposed to stop by and pick up her cousin Rosemary, who was only a freshman and take her to the dance at Wilson High that evening. But Miranda had plans to meet cute Robbie Coopers for a coke and walk over to the school with him. No way was she going to drag Rosemary, who still wore clothes suitable only for a grade-schooler and never had much to say, along with them.

Later, when her mother found out, she was not amused. To say the least. Miranda was grounded for a month.

For as long as she could remember, Miranda knew her mother had a real thing about loyalty to family. It wasn't until she was in her teens, though, that her Aunt Judy explained why.

When in her early twenties, Paula met her husband-to-be, Peter, while on a trip to Boston. Peter Patel was a handsome, first-generation Italian, his parents having emigrated after the War. Ethnic wasn't yet in, so they had shortened Pescatelli to a more American version and studied English, but they always spoke Italian at home.

Paula and Peter had had the proverbial whirlwind romance and decided to get married before a justice of the peace in Boston before they moved as a newly-married couple back to DC. Judy was a little miffed, she had admitted to Miranda when Paula called to tell her. Though she was delighted because Paula sounded so happy, it just wasn't fitting that the marriage would occur before anyone in the family had even met the man. She did not say this to Paula, but when she put Peter on the phone, he sounded so arrogant, and when she tried to ask him a few questions about their plans he cut her off, dismissively. Fairly or not, Judy had said, she was furious. And she never got over it. Paula's other sister, Becky, took Judy's side. The sisters were still happy to entertain Paula alone, but they did not want to have anything to do with Peter.

Peter drifted away shortly after Miranda was born. Miranda's mother got a job teaching at the exclusive Sidwell Friends high school down the street. She had been lucky, her mother had told Miranda. Just a teacher's salary, but as a private school, Sidwell paid substantially better than the public schools. Money in the household was always tight, but not scarce.

Miranda knew that her mother and father were divorced, of course. When she was old enough to worry about it, maybe five or so, her mother assured her it had nothing to do with Miranda. He had loved his little girl, her mother had said, and called you his 'bambina cara,' his beautiful girl. Her mother assured Miranda that she and Peter had been very much in love, too, but the married version just did not work out.

Peter disappeared from their lives. When Miranda asked, her mother said she and her ex never corresponded and she had no idea where he was. Italy, for all she knew. Her mother never seemed all that concerned about it, at least as far as Miranda could tell. She said she had gotten Miranda and the house, and the rest of her family and that was all that mattered.

When she was growing up, Miranda's extended family had a meal together almost every weekend. They gathered in Miranda's home in Cleveland Park or at Judy's or Becky's, Paula's sisters, both of whom lived with their husbands and children in nearby Bethesda. It always took four or five phone calls during the week to sort out the details for their get-togethers, Miranda noticed, although she supposed her mom called her sisters to consult on other things in their lives than menus. Miranda grew up playing card games and riding bikes and taking the metro to the movies, when they got older, with one or more of her six cousins, their respective school friends also in tow.

Miranda sighed. Pulling herself from her reverie, she glanced at her watch. Plenty of time to make her next meeting for the afternoon. Then she would head home. And maybe call Jessica.

●　　　●　　　●　　　●　　　●

Will maneuvered his Prius through the tight fit into the garage. Gathering up his old leather briefcase and two deposition transcripts he had not been able to cram into the bulging bag, he closed the garage door and unlocked the lower level door to his house.

"Norma, I'm home," he called as he crossed the room and started up the stairs. He glanced at his watch and grimaced. Nine o'clock. The only good thing about working late so often, he thought, was avoiding rush hour traffic. Otherwise, it would be a too-hasty dinner and not enough time with his wife before he climbed into bed with a transcript to finish preparing for the 8:00 deposition in the morning. Marlon kept telling him he worked too hard. The other lawyers rarely stayed late unless they were in trial. For some reason Miranda had also become a late bird, Will had noticed, but presumably, she would go back to her usual hours one day.

Will was the only one of them who'd gone to law school at night. Though he had been practicing law now for almost three decades, he could not shake the feeling that he still had to prove himself.

Norma met him as he reached the top of the stairs. She leaned into his embrace as he stroked her long, glossy hair. A wave of desire flooded through him. No, he said to himself sternly. The depositions had to be read tonight.

He stepped back from the hug but kept her in his grasp, both hands resting lightly on her shoulders. "How was your day, sweetheart?" he asked.

"Fine. There's much to learn about how this office runs. I don't know my team members well enough yet. But the work is good."

"You, my dear, are good at your work," Will smiled. Taking her hand, he steered them gently towards the kitchen. "I need a beer!"

As he opened the refrigerator door, Will opened his mouth to tell his wife about his interview with Jessica. But then he stopped himself. Will was always talking about his cases at home. He was tired. Norma looked preoccupied. No shop talk, he decided.

Will glanced across the open floor space of the main level of his home to the living room adjoining the kitchen. As always, his thoughts turned, just for a moment, to Claire, the woman who had designed the room. Lush lines and bright colors. The back and arms of the Italian sofas – upholstered in blood-red – curved upward and outward, respectively, in matching plump ovals. The canary-yellow chaise-lounge arched upward at its center, forming a symmetrical bridge over its legs of stainless-steel tubes. Five large windows, un-curtained, dominated the east wall of the room, suffused with the warming light of the late summer evening. He loved the home his first wife had created. And Norma claimed she was perfectly happy with the décor. But they had been married six months now. It was time to make this their own home. Someday soon, when he and Norma were not both working so hard, Will decided, they would get started.

Will popped the cap off his Corona and leaned back onto the granite counter by the frig. Catty-corner across from him, Norma picked up a wine glass sitting next to the sink. Will noticed the glass was almost empty of the red wine that had recently filled it, leaving its tell-tale red lacing behind. "How long have you been home?" he asked her.

"Not long. Maybe fifteen minutes."

She had gone right to the bottle, then. So had he, Will supposed. But he did worry about her drinking. Not that he had ever seen her worse than a little tipsy. But she was new to town and knew few people outside work. She worked long hours and traveled often on business. She had no interest in joining a health club or gym. That she enjoyed wine was to be expected. She was Spanish in origin and habits. Will just hoped she wasn't overdoing out of a combination of boredom and stress.

"Are you having anything to eat?" Norma asked.

"Just a bite of something. Join me?"

"Yes, something light for me, too."

They suited each other in large things and small, Will thought, removing Manchego cheese and Kalamata olives, figs and grapes from the frig and handing them to Norma, who prepared the counter where they would perch on bar stools and eat. They liked the same foods, even sardines, which his first wife, Claire, would not touch. He was a gym rat, unlike Norma, but they both enjoyed wandering around D.C., walking for miles sometimes, popping in and out of museums and boutiques, checking out the weekend events on the Mall. They were both heavily invested in their careers.

Will got up from the counter. "I think one more beer and then to work," he said.

Norma's cell phone rang. She looked at the incoming number on the screen, picked up the phone, and said, "Hola, Papa." She stood, smiled at Will, and retreated into the living room to talk to her father in Mexico City.

Will had taken Spanish in college. He had managed to get around okay when he took a trip to Madrid a couple of years ago. But he understood only a word or two of a conversation between native speakers of the language. Norma's English was perfect, almost unaccented. Will was always impressed by the fact that Norma was truly bilingual and wished he had learned a foreign language in school.

Will had had a shot at the kind of school in which the study of a foreign language was required. His father had campaigned to get Will into Gilman High School. One of the best private schools in the city.

Will had first become aware of his father's dream when he heard his mother and father talking about it at the kitchen table, sometime during the beginning of sixth grade. His mother was arguing that there was no reason Will should not just continue in Catholic schools, as his older brother Bobbie had. Any one of them in Baltimore City was perfectly good, she had said. And besides, there was no possible way they could afford the tuition at a private school. The Church would subsidize Catholic school tuition for its parishioners but not for private, parochial schools.

But Will got straight A's on his report cards, his father, Matt, had rejoined. He kept up with the best students. Will would need more than brains to make it in the big leagues, though, Matt argued. He would need some polish, first. A Gilman diploma. And then he would go far. Maybe even Harvard Law School, Matt had marveled. For sure out of Baltimore, anyway. Matt would find a way to get Matt in. On a full scholarship.

Their family did not move in the same circles as those people did, however. The Gilman alumnae sitting on its board of overseers or writing the recommendations for admission for the sons of their upper-middle-class neighbors.

Will's father was a mailman. Matt told Will he had done other work, in construction and on the docks, before he landed this dream job. Secure, well-paying for someone without a college education who had inherited nothing from his folks, a respectable occupation. Getting the job had been a real close call, Matt had told his son. Matt had had a bout of polio when he was a boy and had a pronounced limp. His mother had been skeptical about him even applying, given that he would have to pass a rigorous physical exam to qualify as a mailman. Will had asked his father how he had managed to get the job, given his condition. Matt had laughed and said it turned out he went to the same church as the guy giving the exam. They had stood side-by-side ladling chili at the annual soup supper fundraiser. They had worked it out.

Matt did not let his buddy down. As the years passed, he walked the miles of his route without fail and without complaining, even when it was cold and snowy, pouring rain, or blazing hot. When he got home at the end of the day, though, the family knew to leave him be. Matt had to settle heavily into his armchair, feet up on the ottoman, and rest for a half-hour or so, eyes closed.

To get Will into Gilman, Matt set out to meet the right people. He joined the Rotary Club and the Lions Club, in neither of which he found any of his old friends from the Knights of Columbus. He took bologna sandwiches every workday so he could swing lunch at one of the country clubs on Saturdays. He bought a menswear magazine for the first time in his life, pawed through mountains of rumbled shirts and pants and jackets at thrift stores and Goodwill, and brought home upgrades to his wardrobe, appropriately fitted for him by his reluctant wife. He spent hours on Sundays, after early Mass, reading in the big public library, looking for what exactly Matt never knew. Matt did not talk much to the family about his campaign. But he was sure gone a lot more than he used to be.

His father helped Will fill out his applications to Gilman for admission and financial aid during the fall of senior year. Will was surprised at his father's confident and thorough instructions. Though his mother had kept reminding him that he should not get his hopes up, Will could not help but feel it happening. Just a little.

Will did not get into Gilman. His father's face fell when Will told him what the letter said. But then Matt hitched up a tight little grin. "We tried, son. That's what matters." His mother said nothing about it. For dinner the next night, though, she served them crab cakes from Phillips, the famed seafood restaurant in the Inner Harbor, instead of the usual fish sticks from a box for the meatless Friday dinner required of Catholics. And she had baked a cake. German chocolate. Matt's favorite.

Will realized, suddenly, that Norma's voice had become strained. A few minutes later, she ended the call and looked up at him. A tear had started down one cheek. "Oh, Will, Mama's had a heart attack. I have to go home. Now."

Will crossed to her quickly and wrapped his arms around her, stroking her back. "I'm so sorry, sweetheart." He leaned back from the embrace, arms still encircling his wife. "She'll come through this, I'm sure of it. I'll call the emergency number for my travel agent. You get ready to go."

Will abandoned all work plans. After securing a ticket to Mexico City for early the next morning, he sat on the bed watching Norma pack, doing his best to comfort her. It was going to be a long night.

•　　•　　•　　•　　•

She should have called earlier, she supposed. Jessica would surely still be up at 9:30, though. Her interview with Will would have taken hours. Miranda walked back into the kitchen and grabbed her phone.

Jessica answered the first ring. Well yeah, Miranda thought quickly, she would have the phone at hand at all times. For safety.

"Hi, this is Jessica."

"Hi, it's Miranda." For a minute, she could not think of anything else to say. "How are you?" Well, that's lame, she chided herself.

"Tired," Jessica replied. "Will just left," she continued. "Well, almost an hour ago now. He really grilled me, of course. In his super-nice way, but still …"

"Yeah. Listen, I'm sorry I didn't give you a heads-up that Aaron agreed to look into a possible case. I was supposed to. Just slipped my mind."

"Oh, it doesn't matter, Miranda. The only thing that matters is that he's doing it, you know."

"Right," Miranda agreed. "So, are you too tired to talk? I didn't have anything specific to say. Just checking in."

Jessica did not respond immediately. Which was fine, Miranda told herself. But then the answer came back.

"No, I'm fine. I'd like to talk, actually. Let's just make it about anything other than me. Even the Nats' new pitcher would do."

Miranda laughed. She knew Jessica did not give a hoot about the city's professional baseball team. "Well, tell me how your parents are doing?"

They talked for over an hour.

Chapter 5

Thursday morning at 11:00, Will called the lawyers to Aaron's office to report on his interview with Jessica and the follow-up work he had done, with Jim's help. Aaron was out of the office at a Bar committee meeting

"We taped and transcribed the interview, so you can read the whole thing if you want. But here are the highlights. Before she got the job at McKinsey, she worked six months or so for Paul Loeb's firm. You guys all know Paul is Aaron's brother-in-law, right?"

Heads nodded. Paul was a tax attorney. Tax attorneys did not frequent courtrooms or doctors' offices, as med mal lawyers did. Their paths did not cross during the business day. But everyone had been introduced to Paul at some banquet or another, charitable events selling expensive tickets to support some worthy cause. Aaron regularly bought tables at these events, which his lawyers were expected to fill. His wife's brother, Paul, often took one of the seats.

Will continued. "Before Paul's firm, and after she graduated from Johns Hopkins' School of Advanced International Studies, Jessica got a job working as an analyst with the NSA. It was her 'dream job,' Jessica said. The work was challenging, she was looking forward to traveling a lot, and she felt like she was making a difference. Making a contribution to national security. Anyway, she was very proud of what she was doing."

"Which was what, exactly?" Betsy asked. "I suspect if we're going to find any clue to what happened to Jessica it may be hidden deep in the weeds. The details, that is."

Betsy rarely spoke at the lawyers' meetings. She would answer a direct question but did not often engage in the discussions or the casual repartee that arose when Aaron missed a meeting or was on the phone during the ones he attended. When Betsy came to the firm a year ago, she struck Miranda as awfully snobby. An Ivy-Leaguer, whose previous job had been at one of the big, well-known corporate law firms, Betsy seemed at first to think herself superior to the other lawyers. But Betsy turned out to be a terrific lawyer, a hard worker, and quick learner, and always willing to chip in when someone was behind on a deadline. Which wasn't a rare occasion. She was also perfectly nice, even though she did not go out drinking with the rest of them. Miranda figured that Betsy, who was an undergraduate at MIT and majored in physics, was probably doing quadratic equations in her head, or something, during the lawyers' meetings. You had to do something to occupy yourself with something, for sure.

"It took a lot to get that out of her. I told her she would not violate the terms of her top-secret security clearance by telling me, because of the attorney-client privilege. But I had to let her read the D.C. Circuit case on the point before she'd open up. She took the need for secrecy at the NSA very seriously. She was working on tracking down hackers, allegedly Russian, who were interfering with our military drone strikes. She was not the data or the software expert but the Russian expert. You remember she studied abroad in both Crimea and Russia, and her Russian is top-notch. Anyway, everything was going well, but then, abruptly, the NSA downsized. I didn't think government security agencies ever downsized, at least not since 9/11. But I guess it happens. She was given a good reference, though, and landed the law firm job very quickly. The law firm was always going to be temporary, though. Paul needed someone short-term for a big transfer pricing case involving a Russian supplier."

"OK, so far, we've got Russian hackers and NSA spymasters as candidates for bashing Jessica in the head," Cassandra pitched in. "Did you find any more specific information?"

"It's the CIA who are the spymasters, Cassandra, not the NSA," Marlon interrupted to correct her."

"Oh, shut up," Cassandra responded, but with a smile. Marlon could be a real martinet, always correcting everybody's grammar, but he was also terribly funny and could drink the rest of them under the table. He was also loyal and a superb litigator.

"Not much, unfortunately," Will continued. "We'd have to move heaven and earth to get her personnel files from the NSA. And even if we got them, everything would be redacted except her name, presumably. I talked to Paul, not because he could conceivably have had anything to do with hurting Jessica, but because I thought he might have some idea where to turn. Nada."

"What about her old calendar, the one she mentioned last Friday?" Marlon asked. "It occurred to me it might have a final entry for the day she ended up in the hospital that might tell us something."

"Occurred to me, too," Will responded. The last entry, untimed, is 'the boss.'"

"An actual clue," Cassandra crowed, excitedly.

"Well, maybe," Will said. "If it means something important. I don't know what that something is. Jessica doesn't either. Remember, she has no recollection of that day at all. I figured it must have been her new boss at McKinsey since she was going to start working there. The HR people were very helpful, but Jessica was not scheduled to meet with anybody at McKinsey that day. It wasn't Paul. I tried her supervisor at the NSA. I was told he had resigned. They claimed not to have any forwarding address. Who knows if that's true or not, but the NSA is a dead end. Jim googled him and tried whatever else he does to track people down, but no luck."

"Did you ask Jessica if she knows where he is now? My bad: I'm just assuming it was a 'he,'" Miranda said.

"Yeah, a man," Will responded. "Deren something. Can't think of it just now. It's in my interview notes. Anyway, Jessica has no idea. She didn't know he'd resigned, either."

"Maybe it was someone she didn't know. Had never met. That might explain why she just wrote 'the boss.'" Miranda suggested.

"Could be, but that doesn't get us anywhere," Marlon noted.

"All these secrets and spies. Spooks. Whatever. Maybe she found out something she wasn't supposed to know," Cassandra offered. "And because of that, she was a threat to someone. Or something."

"And so, to eliminate the threat, they poisoned Jessica," Miranda said.

Jaws dropped.

"What in the world are you talking about," Marlon asked?

Miranda recounted her conversation with Dr. Franklin. Everyone sat still for a moment, thinking.

"Wait, wait, you guys." Marlon stood and walked over to the east windows, looking out at the storm clouds gathering over D.C., the dome of the Capitol rising above the downtown office buildings. "How many people in this town work for some secretive government agency or the other? Thousands, surely. And how many end up near death because of what they do? A handful, maybe, because they were working in South Sudan or somewhere like that. Remember Occam's razor. The simplest answer is usually the right answer. From what Dr. Franklin said, it seems most likely that Jessica bumped her head, possibly in some kind of an accident."

"You're right," Will said. He smiled. "As usual," he continued. "The surgeon is in the clear, but we don't know yet about the other care Jessica received. We just wait to see what the experts say about that."

"Yeah, I get it," Miranda said. "But you know there's a very slim chance that we have any malpractice, once Dr. Franklin cleared the surgery. And what if we don't have any malpractice? What then? Jessica may have had an accident caused by someone else, you know. If we can't sue the hospital or the ambulance service, we might still have an alternative defendant. And we should be looking for him. Or her. Just in case. Jessica doesn't have much time."

"I thought you didn't have time to spend on Jessica's case," Marlon said, looking at Miranda, eyebrows raised. "You didn't want to take the lead. What's up?"

Miranda waved her hand, brushing off the question. "I'm right, aren't I?" she asked.

"Well," Marlon responded. "Yes and no. Mostly no, actually," he corrected himself.

Marlon explained. It was certainly possible that Jessica went out to dinner or elsewhere with someone that night. Jessica's companion accidentally bumped into her on the way into a restaurant and Jessica hit her head on the door. Or he drove her home after dinner or a play and had a fender bender. And he would not have known anything was wrong with Jessica at first because Jessica bled slowly. She would not have had any noticeable symptoms for hours.

"But even if it happened that way, we'll never find this supposed person," he concluded.

"Why are you so sure," Miranda asked.

"Because anybody close enough to Jessica to be a dinner date would surely have followed up the next day and found out Jessica was in the hospital on death's door. Would have wondered if a little bump on the head could possibly have been the cause. Would have doubted it. But would have at least shown up and explained to the doctors what had happened. Just in case he was responsible in any way. Didn't happen."

"Ah, got it," Cassandra chimed in. "The other possible candidate to sue is a friend who isn't about to admit anything happened. Or a one-time blind date who either didn't call Jessica the next day to thank her for a lovely evening or called and, not getting any response, after a few days forgot about it."

"Sums it up," Marlon admitted. "And though I hate to put any more roadblocks in the way of your investigation, Miranda, there's another thing. As I said earlier, I'm strongly doubting the poisoning by the NSA to keep Jessica from disclosing secrets. But Jessica might have been assaulted by a common criminal, you know. I know the police didn't find anything like that, but I'm guessing they didn't look all that hard. They don't have much time to spend on an isolated crime like that, particularly if the victim survived. And even though we could bring a civil suit for the damages caused by the assault, that's not going to happen. We're never going to find that guy, either."

"You're just so sure," Miranda glared at Marlon. "But what if you're wrong? Wrong about all of it? We just give up if we don't find med mal, and Jessica stays in a wheelchair? Or maybe she's still a threat to somebody, and something even worse will happen to her. Or ..."

"Miranda," Will interrupted. "Crusading for Jessica is admirable ..."

"I'm doing no such thing," Miranda broke in, impatiently. "Just doing my job."

"Okay, okay," Will soothed. "But Aaron's going to see it Marlon's way. Anything other than a med mal case is just a shot in the dark. On which you shouldn't be wasting your salary. And even if you wanted to explore other options in your free time, how in the world would you go about it? You're a med mal lawyer, Miranda, not a cop."

"He's right." No one had noticed Aaron standing just outside the threshold of his office. He turned to leave, probably on his way out for a lunch meeting. But then he turned back. "Miranda, we're doing what we can, you know."

That afternoon, at three o'clock, according to her computer clock, Miranda stood up and stretched. God, what a mess her office was. Her desk was covered with opened books, photo-copies of court decisions and dozens of pleadings from various cases, envelopes and letters and who knew what else, in apparently random order and uneven, ragged piles. Her side table bore a similar burden. Marlon, whose ability to churn out winning briefs in a remarkably short time was legendary, had a different working style. His desk rarely had more than one document on it, placed squarely in the center. Miranda sighed. Maybe she would take part of the weekend to straighten up her office.

She had spent a good part of the afternoon reading the transcript of Will's interview of Jessica. Guiltily, given what Will had said about sticking to her paid job. But something about what Cassandra said had gotten her thinking. That bit about the friend who might have had something to do with what happened to Jessica but would not admit it. Sarah Hester had come to mind. She was the only person who had any first-hand knowledge of the events of that evening before the medical professionals stepped in. As far as they knew. But then, once cleared from any suspicion of foul play by the police, she had just dropped out of the picture. Miranda had confirmed that by reading the transcript. Jessica had not gone back to her old apartment building to talk to Sarah since she had gotten back to D.C. Had not had time, Jessica had told Will. The transcript had also confirmed that Jessica and Sarah had been friends. Or at least friendly. They had socialized now and again.

"Lawyers, lawyers," suddenly came over the intercom. Aaron's voice had a strange note, Miranda thought, one she did not recall hearing before. "A lawyer's meeting is called immediately. Right now," he repeated.

A few minutes later, the associates still filing in, Aaron said, his voice commanding: "We have an urgent matter that needs our full attention. A grand jury is considering issuing an indictment charging Paul with tax fraud."

Their usual pre-meeting chatter stopped abruptly.

One thought crossed all minds simultaneously. Marlon voiced it: "Paul? That's impossible!"

Marlon had known Paul for as long as he had known Aaron. Twenty years. Paul was high-profile in the tax bar. He serviced the tax needs of high-profile corporations and worked with top-level IRS officials. These movers-and-shakers had high expectations of Paul's work, and those expectations were always met. With intelligence, skill, and diligence. Never had there ever been any suggestion of any impropriety. Not even close. His professional reputation was spotless. Plus, he was a generous donor and heavily involved in the community work of his synagogue.

"Of course, it's impossible," Aaron snapped. "And, of course, he's already engaged a prominent white-collar defense lawyer from Williams and Connolly. One of the best. But I owe it to him to help in any way I can. I want to help. Let's brainstorm. And Will set a thirty-day clock for Paul. The word is the indictment may issue by the end of September. Come on, let's move into the library where we can get to work."

As they were getting up, legal pads and pens in hand, Betsy posed a question, directed at no one in particular: "How can we know about all this? How does Paul know? A grand jury proceeding is not public. It's all hush-hush until an indictment actually issues."

"Betsy, you just haven't worked in this town long enough. Let's just say in DC information seeps out as easily as water through a sieve," Cassandra answered. "In some circles, the City's called a swamp. In reality, it's a fishbowl."

$\bullet$ $\bullet$ $\bullet$ $\bullet$ $\bullet$

Chad's flight into Dulles, his second in two weeks, arrived at 4:29 p.m., right on time. When he got to the main terminal's rows of car rental kiosks, he got in the short line in front of Dollar. He used a credit card; he could be traced. He did not like it, but he would put up with it. Besides, he figured no one would be looking very hard at data from a low-end car rental company. And he had decided he needed a car this trip. Too many time-sensitive trips back and forth. He could not afford to rely on cabs.

He drove the dark-blue Taurus out of the garage and maneuvered through the madness of airport traffic. Hundreds of drivers were trying to park curbside, aiming for crowded passenger drop-off and pick-up lanes as other cars pulled unexpectedly into or out of the uneven rows. Dozens of buses and cabs started and stopped at seemingly random locations amid passengers dragging enormous bags here and there across the terminal access roads, heedless of the indicated crosswalks from the terminal to the parking garages.

Chad got on the access road towards the City. He had a Holiday Inn Express reservation in McLean. Low-class digs, for sure, but chosen for its easy access to Langley. He would have an early dinner somewhere decent and turn in early. Tomorrow's meeting would start early, and no doubt, end late.

Chapter 6

1986

Chad sat cross-legged on his twin bed. He could dangle his legs between the two beds, the second one just having been brought in this afternoon, but just barely. Ed, standing with his back to Chad beside the scuffed wooden four-drawer bureau against the wall, reached into the cardboard carton sitting on top of the bureau.

"Last one," Ed crowed, pulling a faded red t-shirt out of the carton and waving it exultantly. "And it all fits," he said, turning to Chad with a wide smile.

It was Ed's idea. It would never have occurred to Chad as a possibility. Nor, when Ed suggested it, just in passing, really, but with such a serious look, did Chad even know if he bought the idea. But the more he thought about it, the more it appealed to him. Convincing their parents was going to be a totally different matter, though.

In the end, it was their teacher, Mr. Hoffman, who convinced Ed's mother. The two boys were fiercely competitive, trying to best each other in everything, including class assignments. But they were also supportive of each other, unusually so for eighth-grade boys, Mr. Hoffman observed. A formula for success, he thought. Plus, Ed would be better off in a familiar environment until the shock of his father's death subsided. Everything would be new in Los Angeles, Ed's mother's home town and where she planned to re-locate.

Chad's mother was an easier sell. She had seen the change in her son once he had found a real friend. Chad's father just shrugged and said they had plenty of room. So, after his mother's tearful farewells, Ed came to live with Chad.

The adults did not know, Chad supposed, that Ed had given Mr. Hoffman his script. Chad thought it was all true, what Mr. Hoffman had said. But that wasn't the whole story, Chad thought. Maybe not even the most important part. Ed was trying to figure out his new role. The one without Sarge.

It was a long, cold, and rainy spring. The boys, trapped inside after school hours, played a lot of chess. Both were good players, but Chad almost always won. One April afternoon, sun finally out, Ed said he was bored with chess. "Too many rules," he complained. Ed was just tired of losing, Chad thought. Ed proposed they learn a better game, what he called "real people chess."

"Okay, and what's that?" Chad asked distractedly, eyes on the board, planning his next move. "We direct people's moves," Ed explained. "According to our rules. They will be doing our bidding, but they don't know it's us. They don't even know they are being manipulated."

"Why?" Chad asked. Ed had his attention now. "What would be the point?" Chad continued. "And how would we do it?"

"The 'why' is to get what we want, dumbo," Ed answered.

Chad cocked his hand into a fist and mockingly shook it at Ed. "Okay, smarty-pants," Chad said, "And just how are we going to accomplish this?"

"We'll figure out the 'how' as we go along," Ed answered. "I have my first 'why,' though," he said, sounding smug.

Ed explained. He wanted to trick Ellen, a pretty, popular classmate, into a tryst with Chad beneath the football field bleachers. She would be led to believe she was meeting the Base Commandant's son, George, with whom Ellen usually hung out. She would be appalled to find the shy, bookish Chad waiting for her with outstretched arms, as though expecting her hug. She would be terribly embarrassed if Chad told and would have to beg Chad to keep it secret.

Chad's face registered only confusion. "I don't want to do anything like that," he said. "And why would you want me too, anyway?"

"Come on, Chad, you were there," Ed said, exasperated. "Ellen crashed her bicycle into mine. Bent the spokes of my front wheel all to heck. Took us forever to hammer them out, and that wheel will never spin just right again."

"But she apologized," Chad protested. "And I don't think she did it on purpose."

"So?" Ed asked. "I still have a bum bike. And I sure don't have any money to replace it." They argued about it for a while, but ultimately Ed convinced Chad to give it a try. They would not be doing her any real harm. And it would be interesting to see if they could make it happen.

Their first effort at controlling the board of life was a bust, though. Ed planted the note, ostensibly written by George, in her algebra textbook. Chad was in position as planned. But Ellen never showed up. What exactly went awry the boys never discovered. But they would start ironing the bugs out of this new game.

Which they did, in due time. Their complementary skills – Chad good with math and logic and with appearing and disappearing below the radar screen, and Ed's better "people skills," including exuding confidence and inviting trust – combined well in this venture. Over time, Ed and Chad planned and implemented ever-more-elaborate ruses, involving forgery, voice mimicry, planted evidence, and even some magic tricks they learned from a book Ed found at one of the bookstores in Junction City. The end game was harmless, they thought. A little embarrassment. Some perplexed shaking of the head. This was all for their own amusement and good for their brains, Ed kept claiming. They were not in it to harm anyone. And, they had agreed, their skills at this game might just come in handy someday.

That summer before they would start high school flew by, as usual. The boys swam and biked and ate sandwiches out in the hills. A friend of Chad's mother bought a used motorboat that summer. It was a special treat when they were invited for an outing on Milford Lake.

The boys spent a lot of time sitting on the bench for their Little League team. The coach believed that anybody on the base who tried out should make the team. But he did not like to lose. Only the better players were sent onto the diamond.

In the first week of August, Chad and Ed met with the counselor at the high school to work out their schedules. The boys had one free elective, and the counselor suggested a new class offered for the first time that year. Introduction to Fortran, he said it was. A professor at K-State who lived close to the base had offered to teach it at the base high school. The counselor said he did not understand it very well, but it was a sort of a language that one used to communicate with computers. He had a notion that it would be a good fit with Chad's math skills. And Ed was good at math too, the counselor hastily added. They signed up.

At home that evening, lounging on the back porch in the warm summer evening, Ed announced that he was going to be popular in high school. Chad did not even open his eyes. "You're not popularity material," Chad said dismissively.

"Ha. Just watch me," Ed crowed.

Chad sat up. "But why would you want to be popular?" he asked. Puzzled. A little hurt.

"Who said I wanted to be popular?" Ed was grinning. "I'm just going to see if I can do it."

"But why?" Chad protested.

Ed shrugged. "Mr. Hoffman said it was smart to court popularity," he answered. "If people like you, they'll help you out. Or at least forgive your sins."

Chapter 7

Late Thursday afternoon, Aaron left his associates puzzling over what they could possibly do about Paul. Thirty minutes later, Aaron's driver pulled into the driveway of Paul's modest bungalow situated on a quiet street in Arlington at precisely 6:00. Though Paul was a very successful attorney, he did not flaunt his wealth by living in a "McMansion" in Great Falls, or one of the pricey penthouses in the Watergate.

Paul opened the door before Aaron rang the bell. They shook hands, heartily.

"Lauren said to give you a hug," Aaron said.

Paul smiled wanly. Aaron was definitely not the hugging type. "Consider it done. Come on in," Paul said. Paul motioned Aaron into the square front room. "What can I get you? Tea? Sparkling water?" They used to enjoy a good bottle of wine together, but Aaron had gone on the wagon years ago.

"No, no, thanks. Let's just get down to business," Aaron said, taking his usual seat on the armchair across from the sofa, on which Paul sat. Aaron took his first good look at Paul. He was pale, his face drawn. He seemed already to have lost weight, even though it had only been a couple of days since his world tilted upside down. "What, exactly, are the authorities accusing you of doing?"

Paul sighed. "It's complicated. But in a nutshell, moving money around in my client accounts in a sort of 'reverse laundering' scheme. As far as we can tell, they think I was moving my taxable income into dirty off-shore funds that the IRS would never find."

"I know you did no such thing. So, what kind of evidence do they claim they have?"

"Digital evidence, of course. Everything in banking is done electronically now. Just like everywhere else. Apparently, one of the intermediary banks detected an anomalous electronic footprint that was used to camouflage the transaction and reported it to the FBI."

"What does your lawyer say? How solid is this evidence?"

"He doesn't know yet. We won't get our hands on the actual evidence until after the indictment has come down and I'm arraigned. This is all word of mouth so far. He's trying to get a meeting with the U.S. Attorney, but it's probably not going to happen until the charges are filed in court."

Paul abruptly stopped talking. Slumping forward, he dropped his head into his clenched hands. After a few deep breaths, he straightened and looked across at Aaron. Aaron grimaced, for Paul had tears in his eyes.

"Think of it, Aaron. A tax attorney charged with tax fraud. I'll be ruined if we get that far."

Aaron stood. "I think I'll get that glass of water now," he said as he started across the room towards the kitchen in the back of the house. He would give Paul a few minutes to pull himself together. "I'll be right back."

When Aaron returned, Paul was up and pacing back and forth across the living room. Aaron sat back down and said: "Let's think this through logically. It seems to me we have to assume the evidence is valid. That is, there is no reason to think the prosecution is falsifying evidence. They don't go around doing that. The charges must be legitimate too, in that the evidence supports them. At least that's what we'll assume. But you are innocent. Didn't do what the evidence shows. So, what's wrong with this picture? What are we missing?"

"This will probably sound a little crazy," Paul said. "And I'm hesitant even to mention it. But I think I know someone who might be out to get me. Maybe he hired someone to hack into my client accounts and plant fake electronic evidence against me."

Aaron's eyebrows shot up, and his eyes widened. "Crazy, indeed," he exclaimed.

"Let me explain," Paul began.

After he had related the story, Paul sat back in his chair and rubbed one hand over his balding scalp. A few minutes later, he broke the silence. "Thoughts?" he asked.

"With all due respect, a little far-fetched, I think," Aaron answered. "Although," he quickly continued, "I understand we need to explore all possible explanations. Let me ask this," Aaron continued, "I know it was a long time ago, but was there anything particular that struck you about this man? Anything that would suggest he was capable of doing something like this?"

Paul shook his head, no. "I actually remember him fairly well. Given what later happened, that summer was burned into my memory. He seemed like an ordinary young man. The only thing that struck me as somewhat odd was the Saturday afternoon we had a firm baseball game. It was awfully hot and humid. Everybody else had on t-shirts, at most, and a few of the young guys even stripped those off. Dance wore a long sleeve shirt. Never even rolled up his sleeves."

•   •   •   •   •

The next morning at 9:00, Marlon walked into Jim's office "Where is everybody?" he asked. "Aaron and Lauren left for Cleveland early this morning, but where are all the other lawyers?"

"Will's at a depo in Bethesda," Jim answered. "Kim's on the way to Philly for a meeting and won't be back until late this afternoon," he continued. "Cassandra and Betsy are in court for scheduling conferences. Who knows when they'll get back. Friday morning. Court will be busy. Miranda should be in any minute."

The chime sounded from the door to the office suite. "Sure enough," Marlon said. "I'm going to see if Miranda wants to run down to Firehook Bakery to have coffee," he said to Jim. "We'll be back in an hour or so but call if you need us for anything."

"Good, we missed rush hour," Marlon said as they entered the bakery down the street from their office. One person was at the register, paying for coffee, but otherwise, they were the only customers waiting to order. "Medium, black, for me, please," Marlon put in his order as he reached into his back pocket to retrieve his wallet. "I'll get it, Miranda."

"Do you want to share a cinnamon roll?" Miranda asked, doubtfully but hopefully. She knew Marlon did not much care for sweets, particularly the gooey ones covered with frosting.

"Most certainly not," he replied, crisply.

Miranda sighed. She ordered a pecan biscotti and a small coffee with milk. "Make it cream, please," she said. One step forward, two back, she thought. Oh, well.

They took one of the dozen or so tables in the back. Only one other was occupied. A lone young man in a suit typed on his laptop, cardboard coffee cup beside it.

"So, how was your anniversary dinner last night, Marlon?"

"Lovely. Romantic. Until Aaron called. He's off to Cleveland for Rosh Hashanah, you know, and he wanted all the lawyers to have the latest information about Paul's case before he went. He told me to have a lawyers' meeting first thing this morning. Nobody else is around, but I'll tell you."

He took a sip of coffee and continued. "Years ago, according to Paul, when he was a very junior lawyer, he discovered what he thought was fraud, committed by a law student with a summer internship at the firm. A guy named Richard Dance. Paul didn't know much about him. It was a big firm. Anyway, Paul reports Dance to a senior partner. Dance was fired soon after, and the firm reported the incident to Bar Council."

"So what?" Miranda asked. "A summer intern loses his job. No big deal."

"It was a lot more serious than that, Miranda," Marlon replied. "Dance would have had a record of misconduct with Bar Counsel. He probably wouldn't ever be accepted to the DC bar, and maybe not any other one, either. His law career was effectively over."

"I repeat, so what?" Miranda, sounding bored. "Lawyers get disbarred around here all the time. Why are we supposed to care about this one when we don't even know the guy?"

"Paul thinks Dance may be seeking revenge. Because, as Paul found out later, Dance wasn't the guy. He'd fingered the wrong intern."

"You mean Paul thinks this Dance had something to do with the alleged tax fraud?" Miranda asked.

"Yeah. Hacked into Paul's client accounts, or something," Marlon responded.

"And Aaron buys that story?" Miranda asked.

"He's on the fence," Marlon explained. "Dubious. But he just knows Paul's innocent. So there has to be some explanation. Unless something else turns up ..." Marlon shrugged.

Miranda ate the last bite of her biscotti. "Boy, that's a stretch. I do believe Paul must be innocent, and I can imagine how desperate he is to avoid the indictment. But I surely don't see this as the answer. Sounds crazy."

"I think so, too. If Paul took this to the prosecutor, he'd be laughed out of the office. So, we're supposed to see if we can locate Dance, as a starting point. After that, I guess Aaron would charge into his office and start asking crazy questions. I don't know, but first things, first. See if we can find the guy."

"Shouldn't be that hard," Miranda said. "Just Google him."

"Paul's done that," Marlon said. "He's been looking for years," he continued. "When Paul first found out he'd mistakenly fingered Dance, he did what he could to find the guy. To apologize. But back then, in the early '90s, it just wasn't so easy. Life moved on, but Paul did try searching for him now and again. Didn't find anything. He took a harder look recently, and still can't find anything. But we'll try again."

"Did Aaron have any ideas for how a bunch of trial lawyers would go about trying to find a missing person whose name we don't know?" Miranda said. "And who, given that he is now supposedly hacking into confidential bank accounts, might be into other criminal stuff, too? This is way out of our league."

Marlon sighed. "Of course, it is. But you know Aaron. Never give up. Follow every lead. Find the evidence."

"Well, somebody smarter than I will have to figure out what to do about that case," Miranda stood up. "I'm going to meet with Sarah Hester."

"Jessica's old neighbor?" Marlon asked. "Why?"

"Just crossing the t's," Miranda answered. "I just think …"

"Miranda," Marlon interrupted her. "Look, I'm not trying to be the bad guy here. Aaron's the boss. We're friends. I'll always have your back. But I'm afraid you're just wasting time chasing some other ephemeral defendant. I don't think you're likely to find anything useful to Jessica and you might find yourself in some kind of trouble, instead."

Miranda shook her head. "Oh, come on, Marlon," she objected. "I'm not close to doing anything dangerous. Sarah's a lawyer, for heaven's sake. Works at USAID."

Marlon nodded.

"One of the good guys," Miranda continued. "I mean girls," she corrected herself. "I'm just worried that the malpractice angle will be a bust. We're not going to find a case. Plus, I just have this feeling there's something else going on."

Marlon looked decidedly skeptical. Miranda switched to a tack more likely to persuade him.

"I'm simply being thorough, Marlon. Besides, I'll meet her in the evening, if she's willing. Buy her a drink."

Marlon looked at her, hard, for a few minutes. "I don't get it," he said. "But go ahead. Be stubborn." He paused for a moment. "And let me know what you're doing, okay?"

She smiled. Nodded. And they left the bakery.

Chapter 8

The following Monday, early evening, Miranda cursed as the car in front of hers slipped into the only available parking spot she had seen in her twenty minutes of circling around Georgetown. The story was that decades ago when the plans were being drawn for the new Metro system, the millionaires living in Georgetown objected to having any line come through their upscale neighborhood. They did not want the "riff-raff" to have such easy access. What they got, instead, was a twenty-four-hour traffic jam on their lovely, narrow brick streets because the "riff-raff" and everyone else had no alternative but to drive in.

Miranda was meeting Sarah Hester at Clyde's, one of the many popular restaurants on M Street.

Miranda had had no problem reaching Sarah at her office in the massive Ronald Reagan Building and International Trade Center in downtown DC, USAID's headquarters. Sarah was initially hesitant about meeting Miranda. She had told the police everything she knew, Sarah had said, and surely Miranda had read the police report given that she was investigating Jessica's case. And "no offense," Sarah had said, but she was completely booked for the next couple of weeks. But when Miranda said a quick chat over a drink would do, Sarah agreed to meet her at the bar in Clyde's, where Sarah was meeting a friend for dinner.

Miranda finally found a place in a ridiculously expensive public parking lot and raced to Clyde's. She saw Sarah, whose picture she had seen on the USAID website, sitting at the bar, walked over, and introduced herself. The women shook hands.

Sarah Hester was just a knock-out, Miranda thought. An abundance of glistening, thick black curls blossomed around her caramel-colored face, with its high cheekbones and slender, aquiline nose and enormous, deep brown eyes. Though she was sitting, Miranda could tell Sarah was tall for a woman, probably about six feet. Maybe some Ethiopian heritage, Miranda thought. Sarah was lean but curvy, dressed simply in a turquoise, cowl-necked jersey and black pants.

After a few words of chit-chat, they got down to it. Sarah ran quickly through what had happened that evening, a repeat, almost word-for-word, of what Miranda already knew from the police report. When Miranda asked, Sarah denied having seen Jessica anytime earlier that day, "hadn't seen her for a couple of days, in fact," Sarah said. Sarah confirmed, however, that she and Jessica had gone out for drinks a few times, after seeing each other several times in their hallway and realizing they were neighbors. So, they knew the things about each other that a casual acquaintance usually revealed: Schools attended, jobs and whether they liked their work, recent dates, and favorite places to go in D.C.

Sarah stopped and took a sip of her wine. Shrugged her shoulders. "That's about it," she said. "I'm sorry. But I just don't know anything else about what happened to Jessica."

Miranda consulted the notes she had jotted earlier that day. "What about afterward?" Miranda asked.

"What do you mean, afterward?" Sarah asked. "After what?"

"I know you talked to the police at the apartment building," Miranda began, "but I mean at the hospital. I assume you visited Jessica. What happened then?"

Sarah frowned. "I called later that morning, but they wouldn't tell me anything on the phone," she said. "I didn't have anything else to do with it until you called and asked for this meeting."

At Miranda's puzzled look, Sarah gave an exasperated snort.

"Come on, Miranda, it has to be as obvious to you as it was to me," Sarah said. "It had to be drugs. No sign in her apartment that anyone else had been there. No sign of a forced entry. Jessica's completely unresponsive and with those horrible dilated pupils."

Sarah raised her wineglass to her lips without taking her eyes off Miranda. "Don't look at me that way," Sarah continued, lowering the glass to the bar. "I'm not saying I think Jessica is a bad person. Or that she deserved what happened to her. But I was a foreign service officer. I had a top-secret security clearance. I couldn't take the chance of having anything to do with illegal drugs. Besides," she continued as she stood up and gathered her purse, "I had to leave town while Jessica was still in surgery, anyway. Flew out for a two-month temporary duty assignment in Lima. Wasn't anything I could do when I got back."

Miranda's thoughts churned. She had a feeling there was something important in that last bit that she should follow-up on, but she could not quite pinpoint it. A seemingly unimportant question popped into her head, however. She asked it anyway. "Do you travel a lot?"

"Not now," Sarah answered. "I used to travel all the time. But that was when I was a foreign service officer. I got tired of being gone all the time and switched to the civil service side of USAID a few months ago. I don't travel anymore." She turned and walked away from the bar.

Miranda asked the bartender for the check. She understood Sarah's position. Sarah could not have known, as Miranda now did, that no illegal drugs had been found in Jessica's blood tests at the hospital. But this reminded Miranda that there was a chance, slim though it might be, that someone may have slipped Jessica something very nasty. About which it was really scary to think. But she was going to follow this through to the end if she possibly could, Miranda thought. She did not know if she could have forgiven the old Jessica. But now things were different. Very different.

Sarah had been adamant that she had only a half-hour for Miranda. Given that she would be out and about and dressed, anyway, Miranda had made some other plans for the evening, too. She scooted over to Dupont Circle and, lucky for once, quickly found a parking place.

She had forced herself to make this next appointment and was now feeling that familiar dread. I should stop doing this, Miranda thought, stepping up to the door of KramerBooks, a popular bookstore with restaurant and bar. She would sit at the bar, order a drink, and wait for the guy to find her. But she hated that wait. What if he saw her, changed his mind, and walked out? She would not even know it, so she would just sit there. Alone in the crowd. She also hated approaching a guy who looked like he might be the right one, asking, "Hi, are you Brad?" only to have him say, "you got the wrong guy." So humiliating. He had to know she was on a blind date. "She should lose weight," he would be thinking, "and maybe do something about her hair."

Miranda paused, turned, and, leaning against the warm brick of the two-story building housing the bookstore, idly watched the mostly-young people strolling by. She was at that stage. Thirty-six. Never married. All

Miranda's prospects from law school were married or out as gay. She had met all the friends-of-friends' candidates; gone to the bars famous, or infamous for matchmaking, like the Boat Club; and attended singles events like It's Just Lunch. Failing in any of these, she had tried various online dating services: Match.com, E-harmony, Tinder. She hated the deception, the incivility, and the overall "it's a market" feel of this stuff. But she was not quite prepared to give up.

Her friends told her she was attractive enough. Her mirror told her the same. She was no head-turning knock-out, for sure, but as nice-looking as most of the women she passed on the street, she thought. Miranda had a pleasant, heart-shaped face. Her nose was somewhat bulbous, but not distressingly so. Her eyes were maybe a little small, but the irises were a brown so deep they looked almost black. A touch exotic. Captivating, Marlon told her. She had full lips and a broad smile. Her face, like the rest of her, was, well, a little plump. At least she had a chest, she thought.

She knew she was part of the problem. She was too demanding. Not of the guy's time. She was busy herself. Nor did she expect the date to pay for expensive meals. Miranda had money of her own. It was something else. Somebody, actually. She could still picture him after all these years. Mr. Parker.

Miranda had been in fifth grade, sitting in her first sex education class. Her mom had already told her the basic facts of life. But this teacher was going into a lot more detail about hormones and desire and attraction, followed closely by information about birth control, and it got Miranda thinking.

They were sitting at the kitchen table, having dinner. "Mom, don't you have desires?" Miranda asked. "For a man, that is?" she continued. "Sex, I guess?"

Her mother looked up quickly. "Goodness, child, what do you mean?" she asked, startled. "I mean I know what you mean," she corrected herself, smiling now. "Why do you ask?"

Miranda explained. Her mother told her that of course she sometimes missed having romance "and all that goes with it," as she had gingerly put it. But Paula just had not had the time to date when she was so busy taking care of Miranda and figuring out how to prepare lesson plans at Sidwell and lending a hand when Judy or Becky, swamped with the same cares and concerns and time constraints, needed her. When she got things more under control, and Miranda started kindergarten, those problems with school started. "Remember?" her mother asked.

She did. Miranda could not remember exactly why, but she had not wanted to go to school. She had kicked and screamed and cried when her mother tried to get her out of the house and into the car. She'd yelled "I don't know" when Paula encouraged Miranda to explain what was going on. Miranda had always been a social child, not particularly timid, and accepting of novel places and things. Her mother assumed, then, that Miranda was being bullied by someone at school. Paula talked to the teacher, who assured her she had not seen any signs of bullying and, in fact, Miranda seemed quite happy in the classroom. Paula never did figure out exactly what the problem was. In any event, in a few weeks, it disappeared, and Miranda trooped happily enough off to school.

"Still, I didn't want to do anything to upset the apple cart by bringing someone and something so new into the house," her mother continued. "Then, time just slipped by, and here we are."

Miranda told her mother she did not think she would mind. It would even be kind of interesting, she had said. "I can maybe learn something," Miranda said. "You can be my role model."

Her mother grimaced and rolled her eyes. But she did begin dating. The pattern was always the same. A man would ring the door, Paula would let the man in and introduce him to Miranda. They would get in the man's car, he would drive Miranda to Judy or Betty's house, and the couple would go somewhere for dinner. Then they would retrieve Miranda, and he would drop the ladies off back at the house. Miranda never saw the same one twice, until there was Mr. Parker.

"Richard," her mom called him, became a regular. To Miranda, Mr. Parker looked like just another grown-up male. He was a little taller and thinner than either of her uncles, and he usually arrived in a suit, too, which her uncles only wore to church. Miranda did not pay all that much attention until the usual pattern changed. Her mom asked her if it was okay, and Miranda said it was fine, and Miranda stayed the weekend with Rosemary at Aunt Judy's house while her mom and Mr. Parker took a trip to the beach. Later the couple spent a weekend in New York City. Everything seemed fine, and her mom was even more bubbly and enthusiastic than normal.

Then it stopped. It took a week or two before Miranda noticed that Mr. Parker had not come by in a while. She asked her mom about it, and she said Richard turned out to be the wrong kind of man. But they had gotten along so well, Miranda had protested. Her mom shook her head and said it was best just to let him go. When Miranda said she did not get it, her mom told her to drop it.

It bugged her, though. Miranda decided to ask Aunt Judy why her mom and Mr. Parker could not work out whatever had happened between them. They were adults, after all. Judy explained. Partly because of Paul, or maybe just because of who she was. Paula was incredibly loyal, but she demanded total fealty in return. Any failure in allegiance, no matter how slight, and Paula fled the relationship.

Miranda thought for a minute. "What do you think, Aunt Judy?" she asked. "Do you think that's too much to ask?"

Judy just laughed. "That's for you to decide," she said. "Anyway, don't worry about Richard sweetie. Paula can find another guy if she wants to."

She did, though not until after rejecting several, and not until Miranda had gone off to college. Miranda asked her one time if she regretted giving up Mr. Parker. Not a bit, her mother had said. Paula had done what she thought was the right thing, and she could always live with that.

"Look, Miranda," her mom had explained." "I truly hope, when the time comes, that you find an exceptional man. The love of your life. That you will raise a family and have a beautiful home and spend many wonderful years together. But things don't always turn out the way you wish. You need to have your own life and your own sense of integrity. And the foundation for that is family and friends. Whom you trust. And who can trust you."

Miranda startled back into the present when a tall, buff, very handsome man yanked open the door beside her. "Going in?" he asked, holding open the door. Miranda smiled, nodded, walked into Kramerbooks, and looked around. Holding that smile on her face, girding her emotional loins, she walked up to a man thumbing through a "Spanish for Dummies" book who looked older than, but still vaguely resembled the posted picture of the guy she was supposed to meet. She touched him lightly on the shoulder and said: "Hi, I'm Miranda." He turned to face her and smiled widely.

Thirty minutes later Miranda joined Kay at La Tomate. Whenever a friend was willing and able, Miranda arranged for back-up. Someone with whom she actually wanted to have a drink, and "post hoc" the blind date. For the proverbial shoulder to cry on, or for assurance that her excitement about the prospect would not later be dashed. This time, given that it was a Monday, the friend would be Kay.

"You have got to be kidding!" Kay protested.

"Nope. No teeth."

Miranda arrived home shortly before ten. She and Kay had laughed till they cried about this latest in a series of disappointing dates Miranda had endured. Then they moved on to work. It was something in that conversation Miranda wanted to run by Will. She hated to call him at home at night unless it was urgent. He was practically a newly-wed, after all. But it was not that late.

He answered after two rings. "Hi, this is Will."

"Hey, Will. It's Miranda. Is this a bad time?"

"No, not at all. What's up?"

"I just had drinks with my friend Kay. She works at State. She was telling me about this intense data security program they are putting everyone through, complete with horror stories about internal breaches. Inside jobs, in other words, even in super-secure agencies like State. One involved the NSA. The guy was caught stealing top-secret information and kicked out. This happened a year ago. It's probably a long shot, but what was the name of Jessica's boss?"

"Hang on; it'll just take a second. My interview notes are in my den."

Miranda waited, taking a sip of the wine she had poured when she got home. She had laughed with Kay about those dreadful dates, sure. But it always hurt.

"I've got it, Miranda. His name is Deren Erol."

"Bingo!" Miranda said excitedly. "He may be the boss. The one in Jessica's calendar."

After Will got off the phone with Miranda, he tried to Skype Norma. She was an hour behind DC time, and by now she surely should have left the hospital her mom was in to get some sleep at her parents' home. He heard it ring, for the third time this evening. Still no answer.

Will picked up his favorite picture of Norma, prominently displayed on the fireplace mantel, and sat on the chaise-lounge. He had met Norma almost exactly six months before he proposed. It was a Saturday afternoon poetry reading in Politics and Prose, a trendy, upper-Connecticut Avenue bookstore. Will had taken a seat beside a slender woman with thick, dark hair cascading down her back, dressed in a white linen blouse and khaki slacks. She was younger than he. Around forty, he would guess. She had glanced his way and smiled slightly.

Nothing about her struck Will, particularly, at first. She had a pleasant but ordinary face, with a slightly hooked nose, light brown eyes under straight dark brows, rounded cheeks and lips tucked tightly together. But as the poet began joking with his audience, describing the scene as he had tried writing at the kitchen table while the baby screamed in her crib and the two-year-old carefully poured her bowl of soggy oatmeal onto the floor, Will's neighbor laughed along with the rest of them. With a wide grin on her face, the woman was transformed. Her lips revealed their fullness, her cheeks their saucy dimples. Her eyebrows arched over sparkling eyes. It was not just a saying: Her whole face lit up. She was beautiful, and Will was intrigued. He had not asked a woman out for a long time or even much thought about it. But maybe the time had come.

When the reading concluded, Will introduced himself and got her name. Norma Flores Navarro. He asked if she had time to stay and have coffee at the bookstore's café. She begged off, claiming a prior commitment, but agreed they should get together another time. They both had busy schedules, and it took three weeks before they found a mutually-convenient time. They arranged to have a drink at the Willard.

Both were introverts and less than forthcoming with personal details. But before the evening was over both had the basics on each other. Will told of growing up in Baltimore, getting a degree in biology from Catholic University. Teaching high-school biology in Baltimore public schools, studying for his law degree at night, the first job trying slip-and-falls and then the great good fortune of landing a job with Aaron. His wife, Claire, the proverbial high-school sweetheart, who had been a nurse. She had died five years ago after a terrible battle with breast cancer. No children.

Norma grew up in Mexico City, her father, an accountant, her mother keeping the home. She had graduated with an engineering degree from the Universidad Nacional Autonoma de Mexico and, wanting to see the world, took a job with Gamesa in Madrid, starting her career in the solar wind industry. Norma had worked for Siemens in Germany and Brazil. She had then been lured to the States, where she had never planned on living, by Mid-American Electric, a relatively new entrant to the field but with, she thought, a great deal of promise, headquartered in McLean, Virginia. She did not want to live in the suburbs, so she made the commute from her house in the American University Park district. Several long-term relationships but never married.

Will had imagined, hoped for a relationship. He never expected to re-marry. Indeed, he did not particularly want to marry. He was too old to start a family now, he thought. He had wanted to have children with Claire, but his desire for children died when she did. He did not need any major alterations in the busy and productive life he had constructed for himself. He had read somewhere that the perfect relationship at his age was a woman with a good job and a good sense of humor who lived three blocks away. That had been his goal. But all that changed when he met Norma.

Will admitted to himself later that he was surprised, though terribly pleased when Norma said yes. Marlon, too, looked surprised when Will asked him to be his best man. But he recovered quickly, shook Will's hand and made the appropriate congratulatory comments. They married in a brief ceremony in the smallest courtroom in Superior Court, Marlon, and Cassandra standing up for the new couple.

By now Will had drifted off into a semi-deep, dreamless sleep and would stay on the chaise-lounge all night.

•　　•　　•　　•　　•

Tuesday morning, Miranda's thoughts were abruptly interrupted by the familiar voice over the intercom.

"Lawyers, lawyers. The lawyers' meeting will start in seven minutes, lawyers."

So, she had been thinking, Deren Erol was Jessica's boss at the NSA. He had not resigned, as the HR people at the NSA had told Will. Deren had committed a crime. Treason, even, Miranda supposed. And been fired, of course. Or maybe worse. Maybe he was in jail somewhere, or even in some black hole in a friendly, foreign country that did not buy into the whole due process notion.

Anyway, she surely needed to talk to this guy, shady character now revealed, who was maybe "the boss" of Jessica's last calendar entry. And perhaps the last person Jessica saw before she almost died. But how in the world to find him? And even if she found him, what made her think he would talk to her about Jessica? Or about anything, for that matter? For now, she got up and hurried to the meeting.

First thing on Aaron's agenda was Jessica's case. "Where are we, Miranda?" he asked. "Time's ticking by, you know."

"I'm well aware, Aaron," Miranda answered grumpily. "It took a few days to get the films, but we have them now, and yesterday afternoon Jim Fed Ex'ed copies out to the radiologist for review. I should hear from her in a day or so."

"And that's all we have left, right?" Aaron asked. "The ambulance and nursing notes have been reviewed and cleared. All care appropriate."

Miranda sighed. "Yeah," she said, "unless someone else can think of an angle I haven't." She looked around at her colleagues. "Any ideas?" Her question was met with shrugs, and head shakes.

"I'll sit down with the records index again this afternoon and see if I can come up with anything," Marlon said. "But it's not likely I will. We planned this investigation pretty thoroughly before we started."

Miranda nodded her thanks. But her thoughts had turned to other possibilities.

"Okay, let's run through the rest of the calendar and then talk about Paul," Aaron said as he picked up a sheaf of papers from his desk. Miranda groaned, to herself. Aaron was beating a dead horse on that one, she thought. Paul had a terrific criminal defense lawyer, one of the best in the city. There was nothing Aaron and his crew could do that the defense lawyer could not do better in terms of dealing with the indictment when it came down. None of the associates thought Paul's revenge theory was very plausible. None of them had any idea how they would go about pursuing it, in any event.

"Hey," Marlon said as the lawyers filed out of Aaron's office. "We're all here for once. Anybody up for a Bomb after work today?"

Everybody understood Marlon's reference to the place and the event. The Bombay Club, an up-scale restaurant just across Farragut Square from the office, was the usual venue for the associates' occasional cocktail hour, which often extended well beyond the customary hour. The lawyers were blowing off pent-up steam, and they could get awfully raucous. But they also tipped extravagantly and the bartenders, who greeted the lawyers by name when they arrived, were always happy to see them.

"I'm in," Cassandra trilled. Betsy said yes, as did Kim, though she said she would be a little late. Miranda deserved a good Bomb, she thought, but she said maybe, just in case something came up. Will demurred.

"I didn't mention it before," he said, "but Norma is in Mexico City. Her mother had a heart attack, and Norma went home to be with her."

"I'm so sorry to hear that, Will," Marlon said. "How is her mother doing?"

"She's doing well, thanks," Will answered. "Luckily, it was a very mild attack. Norma should be back soon, is the plan. But, anyway, we are Skyping this evening. I'll Bomb next time. You guys have fun."

Back in her office, Miranda sat down and picked up the summary judgment motion that had come in the mail that morning. She started to read, but her mind wandered. Then the thought occurred to her. Jessica had told Will she had no idea where Deren might be. But that was now, and after brain surgery. Maybe she did know before she had been injured. It seemed likely, in fact, that she had known where he lived. That is, assuming he was "the boss" in her calendar, Jessica was meeting Deren after she had left the NSA. That sounded like they were on friendly enough terms. Of course, turning to her thoughts of earlier that morning, Deren might be long gone. And it was a long shot that Jessica would have said anything about Deren to Sarah. But Miranda could not think of anything else to do to try to track down this Deren. And it would be a simple matter to call her.

A few minutes later, she got up from her desk and walked over to the window to stare out at the Capitol dome. Sarah's secretary had said Sarah had left town early this morning. For a duty assignment in Quito. She would be gone for a month. Now that, Miranda thought, was weird.

•   •   •   •   •

That evening, Chad exited the facility with only two hours before his flight out of Dulles. He had cut it close. But this cabbie was flying down the road. It was after seven, but traffic was heavy. This was the rush hour for international travelers, most of whose carriers offered overnight flights for the long hauls. This guy was nonetheless making good time, dodging from lane to lane, keeping up his speed. Chad was used to wild and crazy drivers navigating around elephants and rickshaws and scooters in the crowded streets of Jaipur, and taking blind, hairpin switchbacks on two wheels on the Turquoise Coast of Turkey. This trip was a piece of cake. He relaxed.

He was not looking forward to two more long flights in just two days. He would hardly have a chance to properly stretch his legs before he would be heading back to D.C. But it was safer than staying. Everybody left a footprint somewhere. Social media alone was truly a curse, he thought. Turn up on somebody's Facebook page accidentally, the guy looking for you is running a continuous scan of the public networks, and bang. Caught.

Chad hated these old-fashioned tactics. They were so far beyond the need to take any real risk these days. But Ed had argued, and Chad had reluctantly agreed, that if they wanted to make sure to leave a trail, they would have to cut through the jungle with a big machete. Well, big for them. Chad could not help but grin. It was low-class but still kind of fun.

Chad glanced out the window and spied the graceful, concave swoop of Dulles Airport. He smiled. Hundreds of times, he had been in and out of this airport, yet its beauty always lifted his spirits. Despite all the hassle and his unease at being back in the States, it had been a successful trip.

• • •

Later that night, Miranda's phone on the bedside table beside her rang. Ugh. Her head hurt. She sat up and grabbed for the phone. Almost ten. Who in the world ...?

"Hi, it's Miranda."

"Can you come help me?" Jessica's voice. Blunt, urgent. "Please?"

"Well," Miranda, puzzled, "I can. But why?"

"I'm scared. Someone's threatened me."

Chapter 9

Someone had thrown a dead rat onto the porch of the house where Jessica was staying, temporarily, while she looked for something more permanent. Her friend, or acquaintance, really, Jessica had said, just someone she had known vaguely at SAIS, was out of town. Jessica, sitting in the living room reading, startled when she heard a loud thud on the front door. It was almost ten o'clock, somewhat late for a weekday visitor, and it had not exactly sounded like a knock, anyway. She rolled her chair to the door, spied the edge of a folded piece of paper sticking under the frame, and opened the door. She propelled herself forcefully backward, slammed the door and called Miranda.

When Jessica, over the phone, told Miranda about the rat, she initially was unimpressed. She had not been to the house, but from the address Jessica had given Miranda knew it was a sketchy part of town. Some kid in the neighborhood was just playing a dirty trick. But then she learned it was not one of the oh-too-common city rats which anyone could have found in the alley and tossed on Jessica's porch. Instead, it was an enormous, white rat, its four splayed limbs skewered to a piece of plywood with three-inch screws, abdomen slit wide open, partially disemboweled. Recently, apparently, because there were blood and guts splattered all over the porch when Jessica opened the door.

Plus, there was the note, nailed to the board along with the rat. Someone had typed: Stop the investigation, or you'll be sorry. Miranda dressed quickly, got in her car, and drove across town.

• • • • •

The following morning, Tuesday, Miranda found Marlon and Will going over a pile of documents in the small conference room in the office suite. They glanced up as she walked in.

"You look worse for wear, Miranda," Marlon said dryly. "And didn't you have the same blouse on yesterday?"

"Thanks, loads, Marlon," Miranda said sarcastically. "Isn't the right question, 'what's wrong'?"

"Okay, what's wrong, Miranda?" Will asked. "What's happened?"

"I spent the night with Jessica," Miranda answered. Miranda told them about the late-night call and her cross-town trip to Jessica's.

"I parked in front of the house, a two-story brick duplex, behind a DC police car. I was halfway up the front walk when the officer emerged from the door on the right-hand unit, notebook in hand, bald head spotlighted by the porch light. 'Are you the friend she called?' he asked me. I nodded. He said he had Jessica's report and he'd checked around. The premises were intact."

Will grinned. "Exact words?" he asked.

"Yup," Miranda confirmed. "Gotta love police jargon."

Miranda then explained that Jessica had already calmed down and thought it through. She had been upset, at first. Shocked, and a little scared. But it wasn't as though someone had shot a bullet through her window. Nobody had accosted her on a darkened street, face covered by a black balaclava, and pulled a gun. It was gory and mean-spirited, surely. But it had struck Jessica as rather childish, too. Still, she had called the local police station, and the officer had arrived promptly. Doubtful anything more would come of that, though, they had agreed. The police had bigger fish to fry. But they did decide Miranda would stay with Jessica that night.

"And how did you two get along?" Marlon asked.

That was a tricky question, Miranda thought. Though she actually thought she was getting a handle on the answer.

The first half-hour or so went smoothly enough. They had discussed the implications of the rat and the note and who could possibly have made the threat. Miranda brought Jessica up-to-date on Deren and Paul and Sarah. Then, a quick tour of the small apartment. Jessica had to make a three-point turn to get from the living room into her roommate's bedroom, where Miranda would sleep because the apartment was not equipped for a wheelchair. Miranda offered to help on the way out, but Jessica waved her off, saying it was just as easy her way. Jessica retrieved a spare toothbrush for her guest from the bathroom and pulled towels and a pink cotton nightgown from a linen closet.

"That's going to be a tight fit," Miranda chuckled as she reached for the gown. Jessica smiled.

"I'm going to stay up a while longer," Jessica said once they had returned to the living room. "I'm too wired to fall asleep."

"Me, too," Miranda said, plopping down on the beige sofa.

Miranda declined an offer of something to drink. The room fell silent.

It was easier on the phone, Miranda thought. Just a voice. In person, Jessica was both the beautiful, blue-eyed blonde whom men would always prefer to women like Miranda. And the damaged young woman with a most uncertain future. For all her good intentions, the former still bugged her. She shook it off.

Miranda's thoughts skittered across possible conversation topics. Jessica sat up straight, shoulders back, but her head was tilted sideways, eyes closed. Something cheerful, Miranda decided.

"You know," Jessica opened her eyes as Miranda interrupted the silence, "I bet McKinsey would still take you on. You've got all the smarts you ever had. There would have to be an opening, of course, but ..." Miranda paused. "What I'm trying to say is that whatever happens, with the case and all, you'll be okay."

Jessica smiled slightly but shook her head, no. "I don't think so, Miranda," she continued. "Lots of travel is required for that job. I just don't see doing it in this wheelchair. I ..."

"But you can, Jessica," Miranda interrupted. "We had a client, before your time, who was a photographer for National Geographic. She most unfortunately became a paraplegic when a drunk college kid unexpectedly crossed lanes on the Beltway and crashed into her. It did take some time, but she did return to her job. Traveled all over the world, and in the remotest of places, with her wheelchair. You ..."

Jessica held up her hand, palm out, stopping Miranda cold. "I just don't think I'll ever have that much energy again," she said, sighing. "I guess I'm more tired than I had thought, Miranda," she said. "I'm going to bed."

Later, tossing in the unfamiliar bed, Miranda tried to sort through her feelings. Guilt was surely one of them. What did it say about Miranda as a person that she had been able to start forgiving Jessica for taking up with Patrick because she felt sorry for her? That was not true forgiveness at all. Marlon was right, she thought. He had told her on more than one occasion that it was past time to grow up.

"Miranda, attention," Marlon said sharply, snapping his fingers, startling Miranda out of her thoughts of the evening before.

"Oh, fine, Marlon, we got along fine," Miranda said, returning to Marlon's question.

Marlon cocked an eyebrow but did not comment. "What does she want us to do? The med mal case seems to be hanging by a thread, anyway, with only radiology left in the picture as a possibility. And with the surgeon, who was the main player, off the hook anyway, I'm fairly sure Aaron would not object if we pulled the plug on what's left of it if that's what she wants."

Miranda shook her head, no. "Jessica told us to stick with the case. I explained to her what we'd found out to date about her case, and about all the other stuff I'd been finding out. She was intrigued, to say the least," Miranda concluded, sitting back.

"'The other stuff' meaning about Deren?" Will asked.

"Yeah, and that bit about Sarah," Miranda explained.

"Sarah? Sarah Hester?" Will asked. "What about her?"

Miranda explained to Will what she had already told Marlon the night before at the Bomb. About Sarah's seemingly sudden and unexpected departure for a work assignment right after their talk, during which she had said she did not travel anymore.

Will frowned. He had been lounging back in his chair, ankle of one foot crossed casually over a knee. But now he sat up sharply and rapped his palm on the conference room table. "That 'other stuff' needs to stop, Miranda," he said.

It was Miranda's turn to frown.

"Look," Will continued, "Aaron, who, I will remind you, is the boss, specifically said not to waste your time chasing after the unknowns. Besides, it's just not safe. A bloody rat on your porch isn't nearly as scary as the decapitated head of your beloved horse in your bed, but it's still a threat. You've riled somebody. The rat may have just been the opening salvo. If you don't stop."

"I appreciate the long speech," Miranda fumed. "But you don't tell me what to do, Will. Not on my own time."

She got up from the table and stormed out, slamming the conference room door behind her.

Will looked at Marlon, eyebrows raised. "Boy, she's sure got a bee in her bonnet," Will said. "What's up with her?"

Marlon shrugged. "She's working something out, I guess," he answered. "Don't worry about it, Will. I'll keep an eye on her."

Outside the conference room, Miranda walked directly to the elevator and punched the 'down' button. She pushed open the glass doors to the building lobby, turned left, and walked briskly around the block. Calmed down, she returned to her office to work on that opposition to the summary judgment motion.

A little after noon, she checked her email. Aha! Sully had reported in. He had gotten back to town a couple of weeks ago and was looking forward to getting together. Miranda called him immediately. She was in luck. Sully was free that evening for drinks.

•　　　•　　　•　　　•　　　•

Miranda stepped off the escalator and headed east towards Wisconsin Avenue. She never drove to Bethesda anymore. It had grown into a bustling metropolis of its own in the last decade or so, and parking was impossible.

She was meeting Sully at Wallis, this new wine bar just off Wisconsin on Montgomery. She spied the name on a red awning over a lacquered black door. The interior was dominated by the bar, a four-sided square, stools on all four sides, two bartenders in the spacious center serving the customers two-deep around the perimeter. To the left of the bar sat three high-tops, each with seating for two. Sully sat at the one closest to the back of the room, facing the front. He stood up and grinned. Miranda smiled and headed towards his table.

Sully, six-foot-four and built like a linebacker, enveloped Miranda in his hug. "It's been too long, Miranda. How are you doing? You look great," he said, as they disengaged and sat. "Karen says hi, by the way," he added. She asked him about his girls, he about her work, and they chatted while the waiter came, took their order, then returned with a cabernet for him, pinot gris for her.

Sully was an old friend from law school. They had been assigned to the same study group the first day of civil procedure, bonded firmly through the trials of first-year law, and stayed friends these many years, though they saw such each other rarely these days. Both too busy. Sully was still a strikingly handsome man. Tall and fit, thick black hair, high cheekbones, and dark-brown eyes up-tilted at the corners. Miranda had definitely been attracted at one time. How could she not be? But not for long. Sully had been deeply devoted to his girlfriend in law school, Karen Henderson, who was now his wife and mother of his two daughters, whom he adored.

Sully had not stayed in the law very long. It just did not suit him, he had said. Sully preferred data to words. He had always been an amateur programmer, and a few years out of law school, he had made the move to digital forensics. Miranda did not understand anything about what Sully did, from the technical point of view, and he said little about what he did at work. But she did know that, a few years ago, he had taken a position at the NSA.

Miranda would have contacted Sully immediately once Will identified Deren as Jessica's former employer at the NSA. But she knew that, six months ago, he had been sent "some place" where he would be working in full body armor, albeit as a digital forensic examiner, and as far as she knew he was still gone. Until she got his email that afternoon.

Miranda relayed her story. Sully was quick to respond.

"I'm absolutely sure Deren did not steal, disclose, or otherwise misuse classified information," Sully said firmly. "Look, I've known Deren for years," he continued. "Played soccer with him. Drank martinis with him. He's godfather to Katherine." Sully's elder daughter, Miranda knew. "Hacking our data would have been like stabbing me in the back. Me and the whole darn Agency. He's also Croatian. We don't stab a friend in the back. Not for love nor money."

Miranda smiled to herself. That was one of the things she found endearing about Sully. He was brilliant and techie. He was a true feminist. But under that veneer lay the shadow of the old world. She could not help pushing it.

"But if some guy insulted your wife, you'd punch him out, right?" She said in a teasing tone.

Sully reared back. "Of course! But that's in your face, not in the back."

Miranda chuckled, and after a moment Sully laughed, too. They both reached for and sipped their wine, sitting in companionable silence for a few minutes.

"Okay, so Deren didn't do it," Miranda said. "But that would leave so many questions. First of all, how could one of the most secretive agencies in all of government be hacked? I would think that's about impossible. And if Deren didn't do it, who did? And why? And you data forensics guys at the NSA must be pretty darn good at your jobs. Why wasn't Deren cleared in the internal investigation if he was innocent?"

Sully shook his head. "I don't have many answers for you, Miranda. I wish I did. But I can tell you a couple of things. First, anybody can be hacked. That's just the way the world is now. It would have to be someone really good to get into the NSA, but it can be done. It has been done before. The agency, for obvious reasons, tries to keep these things under the radar. The other thing is I know how it was done. Not who, but how. NSA's computers are air-gapped. Meaning not connected to the internet. The malware had to be installed on-site."

"So, the hacker had to be an NSA employee?" Miranda asked. "To be on site? Meaning in the NSA building?"

"Maybe, but not necessarily. An NSA employee could have inadvertently delivered malware given to him or her by the actual hacker. Or someone employed by the hacker."

"How would that work, exactly?" Miranda asked.

"Like Stuxnet, to take one famous example. Ever heard of it?" Miranda shook her head, no. "Before the Obama-era nuclear deal was signed, the Iranian nuclear program was sabotaged, most certainly by American and Israeli intelligence agents. Like the NSA's, the Iranian computers were not connected to the internet. That's a standard, basic security precaution, you know. So, if you want to bug the program, you have to get the bug on site. Anyway, those computers were highjacked by a computer bug, created by the Americans, that physically destroyed a big part of the program. The bug was apparently carried into the Iranian facilities by Iranian employees, on thumb drives. Bringing in the drives from outside was completely against protocol. But the drives had porn on them. Entertainment for downtime."

"True story?" Miranda asked, disbelievingly.

"Yep. Worked like a charm. Like most hacks, though, this one was eventually discovered. Not until after the damage was done, but still. In this case, the NSA found nothing. No evidence of a hack. I've continued looking, but I haven't found anything, yet."

"If you do, will you let me know?" Miranda asked.

"Maybe. Remember, I'm not going to violate my security clearance or disclose anything confidential. But I'll do what I can to help."

"One last thing, Sully, and please don't be offended," Miranda began, "but, leaving the hacking aside, something still happened to Jessica sometime shortly after meeting Deren, as far as we can tell. Whatever that 'something' was, you don't think Deren was responsible, I presume?"

Sully glowered, silently, for a minute. Then his face relaxed, and he smiled. "Still the bulldog," he said. "That's why you were such a good brief writer in law school. You didn't stop until you'd covered every conceivable argument for our side."

They both laughed.

"But the answer is no," Sully continued. "That is, Deren would never have done anything to hurt Jessica. Or jeopardize her. You'll have to look elsewhere."

On the subway home later, Miranda wondered where that 'elsewhere' would be. That threatening note to Jessica was the only thing she had now. Assuming the med mal case just wasn't there, she had to find another culprit. And just who else knew there was an investigation at all? Other than the lawyers at the firm? She had told Kay something about it, and she supposed one of the other lawyers may have mentioned it to one of their friends. But none of those circles was likely to contain a threatening rat-thrower. Sarah knew because Miranda had told her they were trying to figure out what happened to Jessica. And there was something a little off about her. Miranda sighed. She would email Sarah when she got home. She still wanted to see if Jessica had told her anything interesting about Deren. Miranda had great faith in Sully, but there was still a niggling doubt about Deren's bona fides. Anyway, she could not think of anything else to do. Not after a long day at work and the wine, anyway.

As Miranda was heading home, Steve Schwartz, Director of the Cybersecurity Division of the NSA, checked off the next-to-last item on his spreadsheet for the day, turned off his laptop and secured it. It had taken him just a couple of phone calls to get Sarah Hester out of town. Now he would head out for his meeting with Danville.

As he stood up, someone knocked on his office door. "Come in," Steve said.

David Pearson, one of the most seasoned investigators in the Division, poked his head around the edge of the door. "Got a minute?" he asked.

"Just one, but come on in," Steve motioned David into the room as he sat back down. "What's up?"

"Something's been bugging me about this project," David, who remained standing just inside the door, answered. "Nothing definite yet, but I wanted to give you a heads up."

"And?" Steve asked impatiently.

"It almost seems like we're being fed the evidence. Not finding it ourselves. Or not exactly."

"And what would that mean, exactly?" Steve asked.

"Not sure. Maybe we've got the wrong target in our sights?" David speculated.

Steve stood up again. "Quite unlikely," he said. "Keep your eyes open, sure," he added, "but don't let up on anything. Full speed ahead now." He ushered David out as they both left the office.

•　　　•　　　•　　　•　　　•

Chad's flight into Dulles arrived at 7:32 p.m. When he got to the main terminal's rows of car rental kiosks, he got in the short line in front of Dollar. He used a credit card, so he could be traced. But he figured no one would be looking very hard at data from a low-end car rental company. And he had decided he needed a van for this trip.

He drove the white Taurus out of the garage and maneuvered through the madness of airport traffic, with its hundreds of cars awkwardly parked, two uneven rows deep, unexpectedly pulling into or out of curbside; dozens of buses and cabs starting and stopping at seemingly random locations; and people dragging enormous bags here and there across the terminal access roads, heedless of the indicated crosswalks from the terminal to the parking garages.

Chad got on the access road towards the City. He had re-booked that Holiday Inn Express in McLean. He would head to a hardware store first thing in the morning and then head into Silver Spring. He would feel like an idiot in that fake uniform. But this would be the penultimate one. Just one of the pawns, but key to their plan. Then, the big one.

This last move would be, on the surface at least, a simple castle: Switch king for rook, thereby putting the opponent in checkmate. It had taken them literally years, however, to get to this end game. The foe was a world-class player, too, for one thing. They had had to accumulate an enormous amount of information, which took the investment of substantial time and resources. Changes in technology alone required alterations in previous plans and the development of new strategies. All this took so much time, too, of which they had little outside the hours they needed to devote to their lives and livelihood.

Last, but by no means the least impediment to progress, was their uncertainty about whether this was the right thing to do. What had Sarge really meant in that last lesson he gave them before he died? They would discuss it and argue about it and decide to put the project on hold. Later they would re-visit the issue and go back to the board. Finally, they had reached a compromise, and here they were. About to end the game. And win it.

Chapter 10

1989

Ed's mother re-married during the Christmas holiday their sophomore year. Ed had flown to California for the wedding, his first flight, about which he had reported excitedly, in great detail, to Chad upon his return to the base. Ed had not said much to Chad about the wedding. But he had not been bothered by it, either.

It was simple math, Ed had told him. His mother had been devastated by his father's death, and now she was happy again. When Clara moved back to California after Sarge's death, she had reconnected with an old flame from high school, and they had fallen for each other again. The fact that his mother clearly loved a man not his father made Ed a little uncomfortable, sure. But on balance, the picture was clear. So, Ed would accept it and move on. Ed certainly believed he could assess a situation, even one potentially fraught with high emotion, as though it were a simple equation, Chad had observed. This time his conclusion seemed sound, Chad thought, though often he questioned the accuracy of Ed's calculations.

Ed spent the summer with his mother and her new husband, Jay Arney, in their beachfront property in Santa Monica. Ed was full of stories about his time in sunny California when he returned to Kansas for school. High on his list of great adventures was the day Jay took him on a private tour of Paramount Studios where he told Chad excitedly, he had seen Al Pacino on set. The boys had devoured Mario Puzo's novel, and when a retrospective of the Godfather movies showed in Manhattan the previous fall, they had persuaded Chad's father to take them to see the whole thing. Twice. And there were the parties with Jay's friends on his seventy-meter sailing yacht, the Tangiers, complete with uniformed crew, and catered dinners at their house where the men wore tuxedos and the women long gowns.

"Your mom?" Chad could not picture it. "In a gown?"

Ed nodded his head vigorously.

"What is it that Jay does?" Chad asked.

Ed shrugged his shoulders. "I don't know exactly," he said. "But it has to do with raising money to make movies. Anyway," he continued, "I want my own darn boat. I want to be rich. We'll get rich. Like Jay.

When Chad asked how he planned to do that, Ed laughed. "Remember, from The Godfather?" he asked Chad. "Behind every great fortune there is a crime," he intoned.

Chad rolled his eyes. "Great plan," he said sarcastically. "And what actually happens is that we'd get blown apart by a car bomb or riddled by assassins with machine guns. And," he continued, in the same tone, "making a lot of money by being a bad guy is just exactly what Sarge would have wanted."

Ed looked decidedly uncomfortable. "I know Dad was skeptical of wealthy people. Eye of the camel and all that," he said slowly. "But," voice firming, "I'm not sure how Jay got started. And it sounded to me like he doesn't always play exactly by the book. Jay may bend the rules now and again. But he's a great guy, too. And he takes good care of mom. So. I'm just not sure."

The boys argued about it and thought about it, but put it all aside when the bombshell landed. Chad's sister was coming to live with them.

After an uneventful school day in the early fall, just finishing an ordinary dinner, Chad's father asked Ed if he would leave them alone for a while. Ed looked puzzled. Chad's father explained that they would like to speak with Chad alone. When Ed went outside, they explained. Talking in turns, in calm, measured voices, his parents dramatically changed Chad's life.

Chad's sister, Charlotte, had been born when Tom was at Cal Tech, dating Amy. Charlotte was a beautiful baby, but she was quickly diagnosed as having a damaged brain. The news caused Tom a nervous collapse, though he was later ashamed to admit it. When he pulled himself together, they married, he joined the Army, and for a time, they tried to care for their child. But Charlotte needed virtually constant attention. She also needed specialized medical care, which was not available at many military medical facilities. When Amy found out she was again pregnant, they decided they had little choice. They put Charlotte in a care facility for children with neurological disorders.

Tom visited his daughter regularly over the years. It was easier for him than for Amy, who had the primary caretaking responsibility for their son. Plus, he could keep the cost down by finding a temporary duty assignment on a base near the facility. Amy was able to see Charlotte less often, though she always made it at least once a year by scrimping and saving where she could. Amy took Chad along when her trip coincided with his summer vacation or a school holiday. Over his protests. Chad did not know any other kid in school who had a handicapped sister. He had successfully begged off visiting Charlotte at all as he got busier at school with homework, and Chad had not seen his sister in several years.

Her parents were pleased with Charlotte's progress. Though her physical condition remained challenging, she had attained almost normal function in her hands and arms. Charlotte had largely been spared, mentally, by her disease, and her reading and math skills continued to improve, though she was always behind where she should have been based on her chronological age. Still, her parents had many times questioned whether the facility was the right place for Charlotte, given that she was able to live in a normal home and attend school, with the right accommodations. But Charlotte was happy. She had made friends among the other children. Her teachers adored the pretty little girl with the winning smile. The facility provided the physical and occupational therapies appropriate for her age and condition, and medical attention as necessary. Her parents could replace the loving environment, but not the rest of what Charlotte needed to thrive.

But the time had come when home was where she needed to be. Charlotte's neurologist advised her parents that she had plateaued in terms of progress on her physical deficits. She would need continued therapy to maintain her muscular strength, dexterity, and flexibility, but this would require primarily oversight to ensure Charlotte continued the exercises she had already learned. And at seventeen, Charlotte needed and was ready to become a woman. That, the doctor said, only her parents could teach her. Her father had obtained permission to build a small add-on to the home and had secured a team of friends and colleagues to help him build it. As soon as it was ready, Charlotte would come home.

His parents ceased talking. His father asked Chad if he had any questions. Chad wondered, vaguely, if he was supposed to have questions. But, at the moment, he could think of not a one. He got up without a word and walked out of the house.

A half-hour later, it was just starting to get dark. Chad supposed he should get home, or his parents would start to worry. But he decided he just did not care. Maybe he would stay sitting next to the fence behind home base all night. Then he heard Ed's voice.

"Chad?" Ed called. "Is that you over there? I've been looking all over. Your folks told me you'd gone out."

Chad hastily brushed his eyes with his sleeve and cleared his throat. "Yeah, it's me," he called back.

Ed trotted up out of the dusk and plopped down beside Chad.

"Did they also tell you we're going to have the retard come to live with us?" Chad asked, voice trembling. "Even worse, go to school with us?"

Ed had known Tom and Amy had another child. He was practically part of the family now, after all. But they had not talked about her all that much, at least in Ed's presence. Chad looked uncomfortable and brushed Ed off the time or two he had asked about her. So, Ed let the topic drop. All Ed knew was that Charlotte was handicapped and lived in an institution.

Ed did not say anything for a few minutes.

Chad's stomach lurched. Was Ed going to bail? Couldn't blame him, Chad thought. He would surely rather move to Jay's. But still ... Chad felt the tears well again.

Suddenly, Chad realized. And gave a great sigh. Ed had wrapped an arm around him. And hugged.

As the weeks went by, Chad realized that his fears had been unfounded. Charlotte fit in just fine. For one thing, Charlotte and Chad looked so much alike, with their wide, brown eyes and silky blond hair. It was like looking in a mirror when he saw her. He had feared the wheelchair would give him the willies. But in no time at all Chad did not even notice it. Charlotte was friendly, warm, and funny. She had a repertoire of goofy "knock-knock" jokes that always made the boys laugh.

Accordingly, the boys agreed, with only token resistance, to help Charlotte with her schoolwork, as Chad's father had asked. Charlotte had some unspecified "learning issues," he had said. Her condition required specialized methods of teaching with which the school's teachers were simply not equipped. In lieu of help from the school, the boys would do what they could. They were both smart enough, Tom added; a rare compliment, Chad thought. Charlotte was behind for her age and would be enrolled with the boys as a junior, beginning the spring semester.

Early in January, Charlotte started at the base school. The other kids studiously avoided her in the hallways and jockeyed to sit as far from her as they could in the classroom. They called her "retard" and "cripple." When Charlotte cried at the dinner table one evening, Chad explained to his parents. His mother said they were not actually bad kids. Just ignorant. Few had ever seen a handicapped child, before, she supposed, let alone attended school with one. But Tom would go and talk to the principal to see if anything could be done.

But that wasn't enough for Chad. Or Ed. They had not expected or asked for it, but Charlotte had become part of the tribe. The boys took action.

Ed had become popular, just as he had promised, plus he had gone out for football in the fall. He quickly got his buddies in line on their side. And when the cheerleaders or the beefy players were around, nobody picked on Charlotte. Chad's role was in the classroom, where he sat next to his sister. If a teacher called on Charlotte and she seemed to be struggling with a response, Chad would quickly raise his hand and volunteer the answer, and he made sure she had the proper textbook open at the right page during the lectures. The boys did not know exactly what was said or what was done by the administration. But, in any event, between Ed's cadre, Chad's protection, and whatever the authorities did, the students settled down. Charlotte became, almost, just another student.

But not quite, as the boys were well aware. "We've got to be sure she graduates," Chad said softly but firmly, as the boys discussed the situation in their bedroom one night. "Tutoring is not going to be enough," he continued. "And we can't do anything too obvious like do her assignments for her. Someone would figure that out, and we'd be in trouble. Wouldn't help Charlotte any, either," Chad concluded.

The room fell silent for a moment. Then Chad spoke softly from his twin bed across the room. "This time, we're going to play chess for a good reason."

"To get Charlotte through high school, you mean," Ed whispered back.

"Yeah," Chad said, "and I've got an idea. I've got a pawn in mind who can't help us much right now. But we'll promote her. With her as a queen, Charlotte will be golden."

"Go on," Ed commanded. And they started to plot and plan.

Chapter 11

Tuesday evening, Mike Danville sent the housekeeper away at her usual 6:00 hour. When he had arrived home at 5:00, he had gone into the kitchen and asked her to make sure the bar was well-stocked before she left. She had said if he had an evening meeting, she would be happy to stay later to attend to his guest, but he had declined the offer.

He spent the next hour or so checking the output from three programs running in the computer lab in the west wing of his house, a five-bedroom, 12,000 square foot colonial on Potomac Ridge high over the Potomac River. When he had purchased the house and its five acres of manicured lawns and gardens a decade ago, the late Senator Ted Kennedy was one of his neighbors. Mike was the founder and CEO of Cerberus, Inc., one of the oldest and most successful data security companies in the world.

He had not bought this enormous mansion to house a family. Mike was single. He did not entertain. He wanted privacy and security. Data security. His data protection programs and systems, many of which he had designed himself, rivaled if they did not exceed those used by Mossad, probably the most security-conscious entity in the world. He should know. His company had been hired by the Israeli intelligence agency and scores of other governments and private companies – those that could afford him – for security consulting services.

He was expecting the head of one of those clients this evening. He rarely agreed to private consultations these days. He would send one of his people when hands-on work was necessary. But he had his reasons for agreeing to meet Steve Schwartz. And it was far easier to do it in his home than deal with all the security clearances he would need to get into the NSA, and vice versa: Steve would have needed to jump through hoops to get into the Cerberus offices, too.

Just after 8:00, Mike left the computer lab, locking the door behind him. He had rolled up his sleeves while working in the lab, and as he walked down the hall, he unrolled and carefully buttoned them. Mike heard the front door chimes just as he reached the central foyer of the house. He reached out a hand for the massive mahogany door and opened it. "Steve, good to see you. Please come in."

"Where's the butler?" Steve asked jokingly. Mike chuckled, and the men exchanged small talk as they walked across the marble-tiled foyer into the den.

"Can I get you a drink?" asked the host.

"Just a single finger of scotch, please," Steve said, taking a seat on the gold-and-white striped divan. Mike poured Laphroaig into two crystal glasses, handed one to Steve, and sat in the chocolate brown leather armchair adjacent to the divan. Steve took a sip of his drink. "So what didn't my guys find?" he asked.

To sharpen the ability of NSA agents to detect hacking, the agency engaged outside experts like Cerberus to devise and plant the subtlest clues of data hacking in pre-designated NSA networks. Steve's people were terrific, and they rarely failed to detect the faux hacking. But in this latest project, as Mike had advised Steve earlier in the day, a Cerberus plant had gone undetected for over two weeks. Mike would not send his proprietary solution code over a network, no matter how secure, so the two had agreed to meet.

Mike reached into the breast pocket of his white, button-down shirt and pulled out a tiny silver thumb drive. Steve reached over and took it. "Must be a tough little s.o.b.," Steve grimaced.

Mike grinned. "It is, indeed," he said. "And it's my next-to-last move." Mike glanced quickly at Steve, who appeared not to notice. "Project, I mean," Mike said. "I'm going out with a flourish," he continued.

"What do you mean?" Steve asked.

"I'm getting ready to retire," Mike responded. "I'm ready to move on."

The two men chatted about Mike's plans for his future. "I'm thinking my main residence will be in the South of France," Mike explained, "though I'm not sure yet." A few minutes later, Steve thanked Mike for his work, wished him the best, and took his leave.

On his way home, Steve made a call. "Did you detect anything?" he asked brusquely, without preamble.

"No, but we'll go over the transcript, of course, and let you know if we find anything," came the answer.

Steve grunted and disconnected. Something had to give. He just wasn't sure yet what, or who that something was going to be.

•   •   •   •   •

Wednesday morning at 8:30 sharp, Miranda dropped her briefcase on the credenza in her office, quickly checked her email, then headed to the office kitchen for a cup of coffee.

"Hi, Marlon," she said. "What's wrong?" With his puckered mouth and contorted cheeks, he looked like he had just bitten into a lemon, or was about to throw up, she thought.

"I don't know why Aaron can't upgrade this stupid coffee pot," Marlon complained. "Our office serves the worst coffee in town, I swear."

Miranda laughed. "That's the point, Marlon," she said. "Nobody drinks it when they are here for a deposition, because everyone knows the coffee is bad. Low-cost hospitality."

Marlon shook his head, rolling his eyes. "Fair point," he said. "So, what's going on?"

Miranda told him about yesterday's events. "There's no question Sully believes Deren is innocent," she concluded. "But they are so close. It's possible even my strictly-by-the-book Sully is wrong on this one. We need to convince Will to talk to Deren. To see what kind of a person he really is. And nail down what happened between him and Jessica in their last meeting."

"But how would we find him?" Marlon asked. "Remember, Will contacted the NSA right after he interviewed Jessica. The Agency wouldn't give a forwarding address, and Jim didn't find anything online."

"Sully will let us know," Miranda answered. "He's checking with Deren first, but he's pretty sure Deren will agree."

Marlon cocked an eyebrow. "Okay, so far, so good. And it's a good idea to get Will on it. If you can make it happen."

Will had an uncanny ability to assess credibility. To sniff out a falsehood, or even a white lie. He once deposed a nurse, a key witness in a case, who testified that she remembered performing a neurological exam on a patient, Will's client, at 13:00, precisely the prescribed time. Her testimony was corroborated by the patient's chart, which had a nurse's note indicating the exam administered just at the time the nurse said. There seemed no reason to question the accuracy of the note, which in those days was hand-written. Will had studied the "13:00" with a magnifying glass and detected no change or tampering. But something about the nurse's testimony bothered Will. She just sounded too sure she had performed that exam, over a year after it happened, he explained later. Like she was afraid her testimony might be challenged. Could be challenged. And that was the only part of her care that she was able to recall so precisely.

Will called for a break in the deposition, which earned him a barrage of complaining and threats from defense counsel to phone the judge. He made some calls to friends and acquaintances, nurses who had worked with his witness at other institutions. Will cross-checked other records in the patient's chart and studied the nurse's employment file, which had been provided by the hospital. Will was pretty sure he knew what actually happened. Through skillful questioning, when the deposition resumed three days later, he got the nurse to admit that she had gone to lunch and had not examined the patient until 13:45 when she returned to find the patient comatose. If she had performed the exam as scheduled, the nurse would have detected a problem with the patient before the situation became dire. Realizing this, the nurse changed the time on the chart. She might not have been a great nurse, Will thought later, but she was an excellent forger. The case settled.

"If you can make it happen, Marlon," Miranda shot back. "Will's told me to butt out of anything except the med mal case, and he's sure not going to get involved himself without some real convincing. Won't you please talk to him?" she asked, plaintively.

Marlon shrugged. "I'll talk to Will," he said. "But I don't see this ex-NSA guy having anything to do with the dead rat. I presume you're thinking Sarah on that caper, for some who-knows-why reason?" Marlon sounded dubious.

It was Miranda's turn to shrug. "Unlikely, I suppose," she answered. "But you have heard the long-standing rumor that the CIA embeds agents in USAID missions. The ostensible agricultural development officer is really gathering military intelligence on the host country or attending receptions at the consulates of other donor countries to identify the presence of known foreign intelligence agents. Or ..."

"So?" Marlon interrupted her. "I'm well aware of all that," he said, sounding peeved. "Actually," he continued, in a different tone, switching to his pedagogical voice, "not a rumor at all. That is, I think it quite well-established that the CIA camouflaged many of its agents as USAID personnel during the Vietnam War. Whether the practice continues is less certain, however. But," reverting to impatience, "so what? Say Sarah is a CIA agent, even though you have absolutely no evidence of that? Where does that get you?"

"I don't know," Miranda said, sounding dispirited. "NSA, a data breach, Jessica warned off ..." she trailed off. "Seems like a CIA spy fits in, too, though I surely don't know how."

Marlon waved her off and started out of the kitchen. "Whatever, Miranda," he said. "Just keep me in the loop."

Back in her office, Miranda decided to call the USAID mission in Quito. She had not exactly expected to hear back from Sarah so soon. But, then again, Sarah knew Miranda was anxious about Jessica's fast-approaching deadline to get her experimental treatment. So, she might indeed have responded promptly. If she was around.

Miranda pulled up the website. The mission director would be unlikely to take her call. Too busy with more important and pressing matters, probably. She would try the deputy director. She found the number, checked the time zones, and made the call.

Yes, the deputy director knew Sarah and knew she had recently checked in at the mission. But then she had gone out to the field. The deputy director was not at leave to say exactly where. Or why.

•　　　•　　　•　　　•　　　•

The uniformed man climbed out of his van, parked neatly at the curb in this suburban, residential neighborhood. It was unlikely the owner was home. In a middle-class suburb like this, almost everyone worked, downtown in a government or law firm office building or out in one of the booming technology corridors in Reston or McLean. But he surely did not want anyone calling the company whose logo was posted on the side panel of the van complaining of unexpected workers in their back yard.

So, he walked up the sidewalk, onto the front stoop, and banged loudly on the door.

Someone was home. A middle-aged man, lean and fit, medium height, in khakis and a polo shirt, opened the door.

"Hi," the workman smiled broadly. He pointed to the logo on his shoulder. "Cable company. Here to replace the cable connection to your house. The one in the back."

"Oh, hi," the owner said, friendly, but a little surprised. "But is there a problem? I didn't report anything. Did one of the neighbors?" he asked.

"Oh, no," the workman answered. "Well, someone might have called," he added quickly. "But we monitor the signal strength. There have been some reduced frequencies here. It'll just take a few minutes for me to replace the cable. Are you on the internet now?" he asked.

"Well, yes, but I could take a break. How long will you need?"

"Maybe ten minutes," the workman said, reassuringly. "I'll give a rap on your door when I'm done."

"Okay, thanks," the owner said, smiling again, and closing the door. He closed down the internet connection on his laptop, retired to the kitchen, and put the kettle on for a cup of tea. The tea was still steeping when he heard the knock on the front door. He walked through the living room and pulled it open.

"All done," the workman said happily. "Should work just fine now."

"Well, thank you very much," the owner gave a little wave and, as the workman turned away, he closed the door and went back to work.

●   ●   ●   ●   ●

Miranda had put in a good day's work. She had needed to get back to her caseload. And she was temporarily at a loss for what to do about Jessica. For the moment, Miranda would have to rely on Marlon to convince Will to interview Deren.

Just as she was powering down her computer, her office phone rang. "Hi, this is Miranda," she answered.

"Hi, Miranda, it's Renee."

Dr. Renee Palmer, a board-certified radiologist, was on the phone.

"Oh, hi, Renee," Miranda answered. "It's good to hear from you. I presume you are calling because you finished your review. Will you be emailing it over, then?"

"Yes, I have my report," the doctor said. "But I'd like to talk to you about it in person."

"Uhh," Miranda stammered, thoughts of the time she would waste taking the train up to Baltimore to Renee's office flying through her head. She shook it. Get a grip, she told herself, this was important." "Sure, fine," Miranda corrected herself, "but this is kind of unusual. What's up?"

"I've found something disturbing. And I'd rather not discuss it over the phone."

Miranda, wildly intrigued, bubbling over with questions, held her tongue. "No problem," she said. "Do you have any time tomorrow?

Chapter 12

1991

Charlotte got her diploma. It had taken just a bit more finagling than the boys had originally anticipated. And Ed's role was as a consultant only because his step-father, Jay, had decided Ed needed some "polishing" to get into the right college and sent him off to a private school in Baltimore for his senior year. But they got it done.

The boys had long phone conversations at least once a week. Tom initially balked at the cost, but Amy shushed him. Early on, Ed talked a lot about the different class of students he had encountered at Gilman. The younger versions of Jay's friends in Santa Monica. Bright, well-dressed, ambitious, with family trips to London and Paris and Vale behind them. They were going to have to work harder than they had realized to break out of the pack, Ed had warned Chad. They always talked about girls, of course, but neither boy called any of them an actual "girlfriend."

A couple of weeks into the first semester, Ed talked mostly about his football coach, Dan Goochman. Ed enthused about what an amazing guy Dan was. Smart, tough on the players, but also incredibly supportive, enthusiastic, and inspirational.

"He's also got integrity," Ed said one Sunday evening, "In spades." Ed went on to relate how Dan refused to put one of the guys on the starting team, even though everyone knew the player's dad was super-rich and a big donor to the school, because he wasn't one of the better players. "And not because Coach wanted to win," Ed explained, "but because it was the right thing to do."

Chad wondered about that. But he said nothing. Ed saw Sarge in the guy, Chad figured. And that was better than okay.

It was towards the end of a late-season game. Gilman's opponent, a local, public school team, was fighting hard. The score was tied, seven all. Ed scrambled and sacked the opponent's quarterback, who promptly dropped the ball. Bodies flew as both teams fought to recover the ball. The quarterback did not get up. Whistles blew, kids yelled, coaches ran onto the field. The adults huddled. Dan broke out of the scrum, looked around and strode purposely towards Ed. Grabbing Ed's shoulder, Dan yelled, "out."

Ed had been accused by a player on the opposing team of intentionally hurting the quarterback. Of an illegal sack that had destroyed the quarterback's knee, ending a promising football career. Over Ed's protests that it was absolutely untrue, Dan kicked him off the team. Ed was devastated.

When Ed called Chad about it, Chad had a hard time figuring out how to comfort his friend. On one hand, Chad wanted to tell him it was no big deal. Forget about it and just focus on classes. But he also knew that, for Ed, it was a big deal. In the end, he thought later, Chad had messed up on this one. Whatever he said, it wasn't enough, because Ed turned to Jay.

Jay said he "didn't give a damn" about Ed's getting kicked off the squad so long as he was getting good grades. Assured that Ed was, indeed, a straight-A student, Jay said he would call Gilman's principal and threaten to sue if the incident appeared in Ed's school records. That would take care of that problem.

The real problem, to Ed, was what to do about his bruised feelings. Ed had convinced himself that Dan had just done what he thought was the right thing. Rather than favor his own, he had given the other kid the benefit of the doubt. But the kid was another matter. His accuser was either a total liar or a dumb dork who had made a stupid mistake. Ed was innocent. But Ed took the hit. Not fair in his books. So, he asked Jay what he should do.

Well, Jay had advised, Ed had two choices. Just forget about it. Move on. Or not. In Hollywood, he had explained, people were superstitious. Smart, creative, talented, wealthy, yes, but they also firmly believed in the power of luck. Good or bad. And if you encountered bad luck, which is what the football thing apparently was, you had better do something about it, because if you did not, it would come back to haunt you. The bad luck would keep piling up.

Telling Chad about this over the phone, Ed said, "Jay would do something."

"And," Chad asked, "just what would that be?"

He had been a little cagey about that, Ed explained. "But," Ed continued, in the lingo of their peculiar version of chess, "we could maybe plan a pin."

"What are we pinning?" Chad asked.

"Not 'what,' who," Ed answered. "The kid."

"And what's the end game?" Chad asked.

"We'll figure it out," Ed said. "Something humiliating and embarrassing. And," Ed's voice began thrumming with anger, "threatens to deprive him of something he cares about very much."

"Don't be a butt, Ed," Chad said, angry in his turn. "You're wrong on so many counts. First, we agreed to play our chess only for good reasons. And that means good in the way Sarge would have defined it. Second ..."

"We can change our minds," Ed interrupted, "if we need to."

Chad ignored him and moved on. "Second, that 'bad luck' stuff is ridiculous. You don't want to live your life always looking over your shoulder trying to find someone else responsible for your hard knocks. Brush it off and move on."

"Okay, forget the bad luck," Ed grumbled, "but remember your Machiavelli." He held up a warning finger. "Crush your enemy, or he'll come back to get you.," Ed intoned solemnly.

"And don't you forget the last Life Lesson," Chad shot back. "Anyway," he continued, "not going to happen."

Back on the familiar ground of their philosophizing, Ed's voice had returned to neutral, his emotions waning. His parting shot to Chad was thoughtful, not angry. "We'll see," Ed said.

•   •   •   •   •

When Ed returned to the base that summer, he sported a six-inch-long tattoo on his left bicep depicting a bright, crimson phoenix rising from an inky black cloud of ashes. Amy was aghast. "I just don't think a tattoo is appropriate for a student headed for the Massachusetts Institute of Technology," she had said.

Chad was neutral about the propriety issue, but he was curious about why Ed had done it. Ed had never mentioned any interest in getting a tattoo. Ed just shrugged when Chad asked him about it, though. "I'm planning on changing my name, too," Ed added. When Chad looked at him blankly, Ed shrugged again and said, "it's perfectly legal. I'll try a new me. It'll be fun."

The boys talked about it for a while, but quickly put Ed's ideas for his new persona on the back burner to focus on more immediate concerns. They had both gotten into MIT, "fair and square," Chad told himself many times. No disguises. No feints. No chess. They spent the summer studying the brochures and catalogs they had been mailed with their acceptance letters, arguing about which dormitory looked more comfortable and discussing which courses each would take to optimize their educational outcomes.

Chapter 13

Thursday morning, on his drive to meet with Deren, Will passed the Eastern Market and its offerings of fresh produce, meats, baked good, and crafts. The Market always reminded him of Federal Hill, the Baltimore neighborhood where Will's family lived when he was growing up Long after the McCarty family was gone, the neighborhood gentrified considerably and, once the Orioles took up their new home in nearby Camden Yards, Federal Hill became a highly-coveted address in Baltimore. But when Will lived there, it was a mid-to-lower middle-class neighborhood of mostly brick row houses. On summer weekends, local farmers set up booths in a small park on Henry Street, selling fresh fruits and vegetables, and neighborhood delis would set up plywood stands from which to offer hoagies and pickles and hot dogs and chips.

To Will's father, Matt, however, Federal Hill was a huge step up from the small flat on the west side of the city where he grew up. Will had heard the story a million times. His grandfather, Thomas McCarty, had owned a farm in Howard County, west of Baltimore. He ran into financial trouble during the Depression, as so many did, and lost the land to the bank. Thomas disliked the city but, seeing no other choice, he moved his wife and four children into Baltimore. Thomas had no trade other than farmer and, in any event, even highly-skilled workers found themselves unemployable at that time. They survived on soup kitchens and hand-outs from Corpus Christi Catholic Church for a time, until Thomas started finding carpentry jobs and his wife, Theresa, got on as a cleaning woman at a bank.

When Will's father told the story, he always said it was a shame the local banker had not been able to do something so Thomas could keep his land. They were just neighbors, after all. His mother would shrug her shoulders and say well it was a shame, of course, but a deal was a deal. And if Thomas, why not all the other struggling debtors in the community? Then the bank would just have failed.

And then they would be off. Will's mother and father did not fight like some of his friends' parents did. With loud voices and hard words. They argued a lot, but they would usually end up laughing together. Matt told Will, one time, that an Irishman had two selves. One was sunny and cheerful and thought there really might be a pot of gold at the end of the rainbow. If he found a penny on the street, it was surely a "lucky penny." The other, when he saw that penny, lamented that "some poor sod's lost his savings." Unlike Matt, Will's mother's default view was fatalistic. Matt could jolly her out of it, though. Usually.

•   •   •   •   •

Pausing on the threshold on his way out, Will turned back. "I forgot to ask," Will said, hand on the door frame, "but I suppose they took your pension away, too."

"Of course," Deren replied, frowning. "I'm supposed to be happy they didn't call in the U.S. Attorney and prosecute," he continued. "But that wasn't done as a favor to me. They just didn't want to air their dirty laundry."

Will looked closely at Deren for a moment. The ex-NSA agent was a tall man, over six feet, Will was sure. He was thin, though, almost gaunt, his face lined, dark hair gone almost completely gray, a sad droop at the corners of his thin lips. He did not look like the soccer-loving martini drinker Miranda described after Marlon convinced Will to do this interview. Will stretched out his arm, and the two men shook hands.

"We're just trial lawyers, you know …" Will's voice trailed off.

Deren almost smiled. "I know. But you believe me, don't you?"

Will nodded firmly. "I do."

It was Deren's turn to nod. "Well, that's something, anyway. Call if anything comes up," he continued, "or if you need anything else from me."

Will turned and walked the half block to his Prius. Starting the car, he quickly punched in the office number on the keyboard of his hands-free. "Marlon, it's Will. Listen to this," and he continued talking rapidly as he pulled away from the curb, into the street, and out of Silver Spring.

Will got back to the office thirty minutes later. He said a quick hello to Beebee, then went immediately to Aaron's office. Aaron was out, but Marlon and Miranda were in their places in front of Aaron's desk.

"Let me make sure I've got this right," Marlon said as Will was sitting down. "First, Deren denies he had anything to do with the NSA data breach. And you believe him."

"I do."

The others nodded. If Will thought so, everyone else would agree.

Marlon continued. "Deren assumed a foreign agent, or just some random kid with incredible hacking skills breached NSA data security, and he was just a pawn in the game. That is, he was just the unlucky entry point, and it didn't have anything to do with him personally. Until he talked to you."

"Right," Will confirmed. "I just guessed it was unlikely the firm would have two innocent hacking victims on our plate unless they were connected in some way. I told him about Paul."

Deren had not remembered Paul's name. Nor had he had any contact with him over the years. But as Will discovered, they had worked at the same law firm when they were young lawyers. Deren only stayed at the firm a year before he changed jobs and, ultimately, career paths. During that year, Deren suspected one of the interns was committing fraud, and he felt obligated to report it to a senior lawyer. He had had no idea Paul did the same.

"Deren was surprised, and then intrigued by the possibility he might have been the target of the NSA data breach," Will continued. "That someone was out to get Deren fired, if not worse, and not just using him as a tool to spy on NSA. He wasn't sold on the idea, though. He still thinks it more likely he had just been collateral damage in a generalized data probe. He'll call on some friends in the FBI and other security agencies, though, to see if anyone can turn up any information about our missing fraudster."

"I'll tell Aaron about all this," Marlon said. "He's not going to be thrilled about our straying from the med mal path, at first. But he'll certainly be interested in Deren's connection with Paul. After all, it seems incredibly unlikely that two people with this same back story would both be falsely implicated in a crime through an apparent hack job unless the hacker was the same person. I'm sure Aaron will want to get Paul in touch with Deren right away. Given his contacts and experience, Deren's much more likely to be of use to Paul in finding said hacker than we ever have a chance of being."

"Heh, people, let's get to the more important thing," Miranda said, impatiently. She felt bad about Paul but thought they were wasting time talking about data breaches and hazy revenge theories. They had a client to represent.

"Okay, yeah, Deren confirmed he was 'the boss' noted in Jessica's calendar. They met at his office. Nothing formal. Just to catch up. They visited for about an hour, and then Deren escorted her out of the building. He thinks it was about 6:00 in the evening when she left. He went back into his office to finish up some work. The last time he saw Jessica, she was walking across the parking lot. He didn't walk her to her car because it's a very secure lot. Fences, guards, and security cameras." He paused a moment. "There's one more thing," he continued. "The NSA hack happened that same evening."

"Oh, dear," Marlon shook his head. "Jessica must have seen something, or someone, she wasn't supposed to see."

"What do you mean?" Miranda asked.

"Look, we now have Jessica in the NSA parking lot earlier in the day she was found at death's door in her apartment," Marlon answered. "She was in that lot at or around the time the NSA was illegally hacked. Sully told you it was highly likely someone had to bring malware on-site in order to penetrate NSA's data security systems. On-site means ..."

"I get it," Miranda said. "Poor girl. I hate to think of it. Jessica alone. In a parking lot. Unexpectedly attacked." She shivered.

"I'm just saying it's possible, Miranda," Marlon said quickly. "There's another possibility too, you know ..."

"One last thing, Will," Miranda interrupted him. "The rat?" she asked, dubious note in her voice.

"Absolutely nothing to do with it," Will said firmly. "Definitely not Deren's style," he continued. "But I thought you were fingering Sarah Hester for the rat, anyway."

"Not anymore," Miranda said. Just before Will came in, Miranda explained, she had gotten an email from Sarah Hester, routed through the deputy mission director's account. Sarah explained in her email that she had just returned to the mission, and the director told her about Miranda's call. Sarah apologized for being unavailable, said she would be back in D.C. in a week or so, and would be happy to meet again with Miranda to answer any other questions she might have.

"Yep, that seems to clear her, all right," Will nodded.

The lawyers then took a quick look at the case calendars, compared notes, and returned to their offices. Miranda followed Marlon into his and closed the door. "How'd you get Mr. Altar Boy to do it?" she asked. "And he went during office hours," she marveled.

"I've known Will a long time," Marlon answered. "A very long time. I know what buttons to push. He hides them very well, but I know where they are."

"Do tell," Miranda commanded, clapping her hands gleefully.

"Not going to happen," Marlon sniffed, waving her off.

Miranda glared, but then shrugged her shoulders and walked out.

• • •

"Lawyers, the meeting starts in seven minutes, lawyers," Aaron's voice called over the intercom at 2:00 that afternoon. Miranda was making good progress on her brief, but she was due for a breather, and for once did not mind the thought of another meeting.

Marlon was already in Aaron's office when Miranda walked in.

"I've explained everything to him," Marlon said, nodding towards Aaron. Miranda looked up at the boss. His face was grim.

A few minutes later, Will and Cassandra came in. Aaron opened the meeting by saying Paul had called him last evening. He had gotten word that the indictment would issue in a week.

"So soon?" Cassandra, surprised. "It was supposed to be the end of the month."

"I know, I know," Aaron sighed. "But now it's not." He leaned back in his massive chair. "We can't just leave Paul in Deren's hands. I assume Deren will make efforts to clear his name, and that may end up helping Paul. But Deren's got no need for urgency. We do."

"What's your point, Aaron?" Marlon asked.

"If Jessica saw her attacker, assuming that's what happened," Aaron answered, "and she could describe what happened, maybe the NSA would re-open Deren's case. Given a criminal assault in a secure parking lot around the time of the data breach ..." His voice trailed off.

"Maybe," Will repeated. "Who knows what the NSA folks would think. But more to the point, what does that have to do with Paul?" he asked.

"If there does turn out to be evidence of hacking at the NSA, given the law firm connection, that finding may give some credibility to Paul. To his claim that he was innocent. Just like Deren did, but nobody believed him at first."

"Maybe," Marlon said, dubious. "Long shot, though."

"I know," Aaron barked. "But we have bubkis right now, people. And I'm not prepared to give up."

"Okay, but you've got a bigger problem," Marlon said, gingerly. "Jessica can't describe what happened. She doesn't remember anything about that night."

"I know, I know," Aaron said, still angry. "But I was thinking about Brenda Korrigan's case."

"Must have been before my time," Miranda said. "What are we talking about?"

Marlon explained. Brenda was a client almost twenty years ago. Her three-year-old son, Robert, had severe brachial plexus. His right arm, which was unfortunately also his dominate arm, hung uselessly at his side. This condition can be caused by the use of excessive force on the infant's shoulder as the obstetrician is assisting in extracting the fetus from the birth canal. In investigating a possible case, Aaron and Marlon identified a nurse, from her hand-written note in the medical records, named Karen Evan. She had been present at the delivery. They needed to find and interview her. The doctor who delivered the child had no memory of the event, but the nurse might. Karen had left her job at the hospital shortly after Robert was born, and the hospital had no forwarding information for her. Marlon checked the Registered Nurses Association of the District and neighboring jurisdictions but found no Karen Evan. When Marlon explained the problem to Brenda, Brenda recalled Karen telling her, as they chatted between contractions, that she was soon to be married. Brenda also remembered they talked about Karen's new name-to-be because, for some reason Brenda could not later remember, Karen thought her new moniker was going to be sound funny. The specific name Brenda did not recall. Aaron called in Dr. Kathy Hammock, a doctor whom the firm regularly used as an expert witness. Dr. Hammock hypnotized Brenda and retrieved the missing name. The firm found Karen

Potty working in Bethesda Naval Hospital. Karen remembered Robert's delivery well. The case settled.

"Hypnosis?" Miranda asked, incredulous. "A nineteenth-century parlor game? I can't believe Kathy would do such a thing. She's a board-certified neurologist, for god's sake."

"She was reluctant," Marlon admitted. "Some doctors do use, hypnosis, though, mostly just as a treatment for addiction. Dr. Hammock, like other licensed professionals, doesn't believe there is any scientific support for the proposition that hypnosis can aid in memory recovery. In fact," he continued, "the studies suggest strongly that any so-called 'recovered memory' is more likely to be a figment, either of the patient's imagination or the hypnotist's. An implanted memory, in other words. So, she thought it unlikely that the hypnosis would solve our problem. But she didn't think it would hurt Brenda in any way."

"And it did work," Aaron said firmly.

"But Aaron, I just don't think hypnosis would advance the ballgame here," Marlon objected. "We're trying to get somebody at NSA's attention. Trying to get them to re-open the investigation of the hack on Deren and, given the connection between Deren and Paul, start looking into Paul's situation. Even if Jessica comes up with a memory of what happened, some hypnosis-induced information is not likely to impress NSA or anyone else, for that matter."

"And hypnosis wouldn't help Jessica any, either," Miranda added. "We don't have a civil case if Jessica got beaned by a criminal. No case, no money for her treatment. It doesn't change anything if the criminal was a hacker trying to escape the NSA grounds undetected after planting his bug."

"People, just stop," Will sounded exasperated. "Stop making unfounded assumptions. That's one of the first things you taught me when I started here, Aaron. Don't just assume. It's good for Paul but bad for Jessica if a hacker was physically present, and if the hacker encountered Jessica, and if he had any reason to believe she was a risk, and if he decided hitting her on the head would get rid of the risk, and if Jessica saw him and so on and so on. That's a lot of if's."

"You're right, Will," Marlon said. "She might have just tripped, fallen, and hit her head."

"Okay, fine," Aaron said, "let's not assume. Let's find out. It can't hurt." He rose from his chair, standing tall behind his desk. "Miranda, talk to Jessica. Tell her we want to try hypnosis. Marlon, call Kathy. Let's do this as soon as possible."

"Wait a minute," Marlon said, sharply. "That's just it. It can hurt. Hurt Jessica."

"But you just said hypnosis wasn't dangerous," Miranda objected. "That's why Dr. Hammock hypnotized Brenda."

"Brenda had a normal brain," Marlon explained. "I remember Kathy said she wouldn't have done it on a patient with any neurological problem, like migraines, or with a history of any brain trauma. For some reason that's clearly understood, hypnosis can trigger seizures or a stroke if performed on someone with a damaged brain. At least, there are reports of such."

"Not going to happen, then," Miranda said. "End of discussion."

"Not so fast ..." Aaron began, but Will interrupted.

"You have to remember, Miranda, there could still be liability," said Will. "We still don't know about the med mal case, but it's not looking terribly promising. Unless whatever Renee found in the records that was 'disturbing" turns out to be solid negligence." Miranda had told the group about her odd phone conversation with Renee. "You may need another candidate for a legitimate defendant. What if Jessica was rear-ended in the parking lot? Bottom line for me: We need to discuss this with Jessica. Remember how Jessica looked when she described that weird, grey gap in her memory? She wants to know. To know what changed her life. To know what put her in a wheelchair. Which she will be in forever if we do nothing."

The room fell silent. After a few minutes, Miranda nodded affirmatively. "We've talked a lot about it," she said softly. "Jessica really does want to know what happened. I'll talk to her. After I've met with Renee. And if at that point it's clear there's no med mal case. Because then hypnosis is the only option."

"Wait," Marlon said. "You need to tell her one more thing, Miranda about the hypnosis before she agrees to do it. If she agrees to do it, that is. She might implicate herself in a crime."

"What possible crime could that be?" Miranda objected.

"The NSA hack, of course."

"You can't possibly think Jessica delivered the malware? Or had anything else to do with the crime?"

"No assumptions," Marlon said, primly.

Miranda was playing hooky. She needed some time away from it all. To let all her swirl around, undirected, and maybe some plan would coalesce. She took the Metro home, strapped the carrier on the car, loaded up the bike, and drove out to the towpath. Now she was peddling easily along the wide, flat path, mind emptied of anything except what her senses delivered. Warm sun, bright blue sky, the boggy smell of the canal, and the occasional plop of a fish falling back into the water after catching its bug.

It was about 4:00, she figured, and few other bikers were on the path. Most people would still be at work. A few riders overtook her from behind, bells chiming, intoning their polite warning, "passing on the left." On the long bend across from Potomac Falls, a rider came into view in front of her. Miranda did not notice much as their paths crossed, except that it was a slender man, middle-aged, in an unadorned black helmet, dressed in ordinary clothes, as was she: sweat pants and, in his case, a black sweatshirt, not one of the shiny, black unitards the professional bikers wore as they careered around Washington.

A moment later Miranda heard the unmistakable, tinny thwonk of a bicycle hitting the deck. She engaged her brakes, jumped off the bike, and tossed it down on the verge on the edge of the canal. She turned and trotted ten yards or so, where the rider and his bike lay entangled in the middle of the path. He was just starting to push himself to a seated position, encumbered by the bike laying across his thighs. Miranda grabbed the bike, lifted it off, and pushed it off to the side.

"Are you all right?" He groaned but nodded his head, yes. Nodded his helmet, actually, as he was looking down, rubbing his bent knee with his left hand, leaning on his right hand, under which Miranda saw blood pooling. "God, your hand." He sat up straighter and lifted his right hand, palm up. Blood everywhere. Miranda squatted down, took his hand, and wiped it off with the hem of her shirt.

"Oh, no, not on your shirt," he protested. "Thanks, but I'll be alright. Here, let me." He retrieved his bleeding hand and gingerly daubed it across his thigh.

"How did you even do that?" Miranda asked. "It's a straight path and flat as a pancake." Miranda regretted her observation the instant it came out of her mouth. Stupid thing to say. Didn't matter how it happened. The guy was hurt. "Should we call for help?" She quickly added.

"Oh, no. Except for my hand, I think I'm in one piece. It's almost stopped bleeding. I'll be fine. I took a call and got distracted, is what happened, by the way," he motioned off to the side where Miranda now spotted an upside-down cell phone. He then looked her full in the face for the first time.

"You know, you look vaguely familiar," Miranda said in a musing tone, still squatting beside the seated man. "Do I know you from somewhere?"

The man gave her a thin smile but shook his head. "Nope. I must look like someone else you know. Anyway," he rose to his knees, "thanks for your help."

"Okay, if you're sure." Miranda gave a little wave, turned, and walked back to her bike. She looked back before she pushed off and saw that he was astride his upright bike. Good enough, she thought, turned, and rode on.

Chapter 14

The next morning, Miranda walked in and glanced at the black, large-faced clock on the wall across the room. 8:15. She had made decent time this morning and would have a good forty-five minutes before she had to head to Dr. Palmer's office.

The square, open space she was in, twenty yards across, overflowed with light, color, and sound. The morning sun shone warmly through the windows spanning every wall, and rows of long, fluorescent lights lined the white-tiled ceiling. The room was furnished with a dozen tiny tables, painted glossy yellow, pink or pale greens, scattered around in no perceptible pattern on the white linoleum floor. Each desk and sizeable swaths of the floor were covered with brightly-colored cardboard puzzle pieces and wooden blocks and teddy bears and plastic toys in all manner of shapes and sizes. High-pitched giggles and shouts from the children joined the ringing and buzzing and banging of the toys with which they were playing. The sounds of gaiety were, however, occasionally interrupted by an unnatural screech, for some of the children in this space could not vocalize normally. These were the sights and sounds of a therapy center for cerebral palsy children.

Miranda had first come to this facility in downtown Baltimore, near the sprawling Johns Hopkins Hospital, five years ago. Her clients' lovely three-year-old son Rajesh was then a patient in the Charles Street Children's Care Center. Miranda had come with a videographer to record a "day in the life" of the child as evidence for the trial. The jury would never see Rajesh himself. No self-respecting lawyer would subject a child to the psychological trauma of being on center stage in the strange and unnatural environment of a courtroom unless it was absolutely necessary to prove some element of the case. Miranda did need the jurors to see Rajesh, to get to know him just a little bit, and get a clearer understanding of his disabilities and needs. She would be asking the jury to award money for his future care, after all. The experts would explain it all and put a price on it, but she also needed the jurors to see the situation up-front and in-person. The video would do.

The camera rolled as Rajesh sat at one of the little tables and piled bright red blocks, one atop another, then pushed beads back and forth on the cords of an oversize abacus. They filmed him eating graham crackers and drinking from a blue plastic cup, and caught his grin and big, milky mustache as he finished his snack. And filmed his wheelchair and arm braces.

Rajesh's mother, Tarana, who was an economist at one of the city's many think tanks, gathered the toys from where they lay around the room or on the built-in-shelves beside the door and brought them to Rajesh' table. He was learning to maneuver the wheelchair himself, but so far could only move it a few yards at a time. And it would have been difficult even for an adult to navigate the room, crowded with other children in wheelchairs parked irregularly around the little tables.

Some of the children were attended to by women or men in street clothes, like Rajesh, but others not. Most of the parents could not take the time off from work, Miranda figured. At least not every day. Several women in uniform smocks brought the food to the tables and then collected the paper plates and cups after the children were finished. Many of the children were much less mobile than Rajesh and also needed an attendant for assistance in eating. Miranda asked, and was told the half-dozen or so helping the children at the time were volunteers. Only the professionals – the occupational and recreational therapists, who would come in later – and the nurse on-call were paid.

Miranda started working at the Center once a week when she found the time. She had to miss as many days as she made it, because of the demands of work, mostly. Sometimes the weather. Particularly at the beginning, she felt awkward and mostly just in the way. Although she had had many clients like Rajesh, she had no experience caring for any child, let alone one who could hardly move. A heartbreaking number could not do anything at all, staring emptily at her when she tried to engage them with a toy. But they tried. The parents of these children, their families, their therapists, and the others. Miranda did, too.

Until it was all over. Children with cerebral palsy could and did grow into adulthood, and, increasingly, live well into middle-age. But many died prematurely of one or more of the deadly complications of the disease. Rajesh, loved and well-cared-for as he was by Tarana, his father, Satvir, and his older sister, Nada, died of complications of pneumonia just past his eighth birthday. Miranda and Aaron went to the funeral, of course. Miranda and Tarana stayed in touch, getting together for lunch now and again. Miranda never mentioned to Tarana that she worked at the Center. It just did not seem all that significant.

Miranda's phone alarm interrupted her thoughts. Nine o-clock. Time to get uptown.

Miranda pulled to the curb in front of Renee's home in the Roland Park area of Baltimore. She had decided to drive rather than take the train as it would be easier to do the stint at the Center using her car. The pearly-grey stucco structure of Renee's house, with its flat roof and large, unadorned windows, contrasted sharply with the more popular colonial-style houses that dominated the neighborhood. The first time Miranda met Renee at her home office, she asked if the house was Bauhaus. It had that look. Renee had laughed and said nothing she owned had a designer label.

Her home, like Renee, Miranda often thought, was just a little different. The doctor was unpretentious and friendly, but she was also brilliant and quite prickly when crossed. Miranda had sat through many a deposition during which Renee thoroughly trounced very experienced and well-prepared lawyers.

Miranda rang the bell. Renee, dressed in blue jeans and an untucked, white button-down shirt, sleeves rolled to the elbow, ushered her in.

"Good morning, Miranda," Renee said. "Can I get you coffee? Tea? Anything?"

"No, thanks," Miranda replied. "I'm good. Just anxious to hear what you found."

"Come on back to the office, then," Renee said. "I'll show you."

A few minutes later, Renee, at her desk, passed a document to Miranda sitting across from her.

"Okay," Miranda said after peering at the paper for a moment. "I've got Jessica's pre-op CT-scan report. Principal finding, subdural hematoma. That all checks out. So, what about it?" Miranda asked, looking up at Renee.

"I think it was back-dated," Renee replied.

Miranda frowned. "I don't get it," she said. "What do you mean, back-dated?"

"I think the radiologist dictated the report post-op but recorded the time as pre-op," Renee answered.

Miranda leaned back in her chair and rubbed her forehead. "How would that even be possible?" she asked, puzzled. "I thought the electronic dictation system automatically records the time of the report. Are you saying the time could be manually changed?"

Renee shrugged. "Not easily. You'd have to know something about the software or have an accomplice who does."

Miranda peered at Renee skeptically.

"Look, Miranda, the chief technology officer at the hospital is a friend of mine. He said the system was built for functionality, not for data security. Everybody's worried about it now, but back when we were first moving from paper to digital, data security was just not a major concern."

Miranda's thoughts flashed back to her meeting with Sully. Anybody can be hacked, he had said. She nodded. "Okay," she said to Renee, "so it can happen. The time on a report can be manipulated. But what makes you think someone did it to Jessica's? And why?

"No one mentions the findings from radiology in the pre-op chart," Renee explained. "Not the ER doc, not the surgeon. Everything was rush-rush, of course, but still, that's a little odd."

"I'm afraid you've lost me," Miranda said, shaking her head. "Explain, please."

"The radiologist made a mistake," Renee answered. "He, or she ..." Renee began, stopping for a moment to retrieve the report from her desk and taking a quick look, "he, looks like, given the name. I think he looked at the film from Jessica's scan but reported his findings under a different patient's name. The wrong patient. When he discovered the error later, after Jessica's surgery, he went back in and dictated a second report, correctly identifying the image as Jessica's but falsifying the time to cover up his mistake."

•   •   •   •   •

A half-hour later, driving back to the District on 95, Miranda reflected on the ramifications of her conversation with Renee. The problem was that, notwithstanding the radiologist's mistake, even if Renee was right about that, there was nothing that would support a malpractice case.

For one thing, Renee had identified the radiologist who read Jessica's scans, a Doctor Philip Glasser, as a resident, a medical school graduate in training. It was perfectly appropriate, however, for the resident to read the films, given that he was working at a teaching hospital. Nor did Renee think it was necessary for the resident to contact his supervisor, the attending radiologist, to review his findings because the image was quite clear, and the diagnosis would have been obvious.

Miranda had seen a lot of medical errors in her day, but not this one. But Renee said it did happen. In a large hospital, on a particularly busy day, the radiology department would be swamped with images. Not, as in the old day, with a mountain of film. Now everything was digital, and the radiologists studied the images on their computer screens. But occasionally the images got switched, and the report was recorded for the wrong patient.

Miranda, horrified, had asked if that meant some other patient had been rushed to the operating room and had her cranium drilled open when there was nothing wrong in there, based on what should have been Jessica's diagnosis. Renee reassured her on that point. No one would be sent for a craniotomy without clinical indications. Observable symptoms that is.

And if, as Renee surmised, there was no radiology report for Jessica before she underwent surgery, that did not affect Jessica's treatment, or outcome, either, she had opined. The surgeon might have been miffed because there was no CT- scan report for his patient in the record. But he would not have relied on it, anyway. Any competent neurosurgeon would look at the actual scan before they cut open the patient's head.

So, if at least in these circumstances, Dr. Glasser's error had not caused any bad outcome, Miranda had asked, why post-date the report? Renee had shrugged. The panicked reaction of a very inexperienced young doctor, she supposed. Anyway, Renee had said, wrapping up, she certainly wasn't going to accuse the resident of anything like this in a court of law. Too speculative. Plus, Renee was quite sure Jessica's care had not suffered even if she was right about what happened.

Case closed, then, Miranda thought, turning her attention back to the increasingly-heavy traffic as she neared the Beltway. The med mal case, at least.

It was just before noon when Miranda got back to the office. She went immediately to Aaron's office, catching Marlon just as he was walking out. "Hang on, Marlon," Miranda said. "I'll fill you both in on my trip to Baltimore," and she proceeded to tell her colleagues what Renee had said. They all agreed that was the end of that road on the med mal case. The men looked pointedly at Miranda.

"Yeah, I'll tell her," Miranda said, sighing. "I'll go see her this evening. But this is going to be quite the conversation with the hypnosis stuff, too."

Aaron shrugged. "Yes, but now the hypnosis is truly the only option," he said. "It should be an easier decision for her now. Though not easy," he admitted.

"The only option for finding out what happened, but maybe not for Jessica's prospects," Miranda said firmly. Marlon had suggested that one of them should interview Jessica's treating neurologist, the one who told Jessica about the experimental treatment program in the Caymans, to see if he had any suggestions for other treatment options. Miranda was swamped, so Marlon had agreed to do it. "Do you have the interview with Dr. Williams scheduled yet?" she asked, turning to Marlon.

"This afternoon," Marlon said. "I'll let you know what he says asap."

• • • • • •

Having started the day early, Miranda left early, too, and knocked on Jessica's door at 5:30. Her mind elsewhere, thinking through the fraught discussion to come, Miranda greeted Jessica and asked how she was doing. They chatted about the news and cultural events scheduled in the Capital City for the upcoming weekend and together prepared pasta and a salad for their dinner.

By 7:00, the dishes were done, and the time had come. Miranda poured two glasses of the expensive bottle of wine she had brought and returned to the living room where Jessica was parked. Jessica looked puzzled.

"Look, I know you don't drink anymore," Miranda explained. "But one glass isn't going to hurt you," she continued. "It's a Meursault. Used to be one of your favorites. And I think you're going to need it." She handed the wine to Jessica, who took it.

"I get the picture," Jessica said. She took a sip of the wine. "Go ahead, Miranda. Tell me."

Jessica cried. As did Miranda. They talked and talked, Miranda, re-filling her glass when Jessica declined a second. Finally, they were done. Jessica had made her decision.

Jessica had just excused herself and rolled off to the bathroom when Miranda's cell rang. Maybe Marlon, she thought. It was indeed he.

"Not great news, I'm afraid, Miranda," Marlon began.

He had had a nice visit with "the lovely Dr. Williams, James, that is," the neurology resident, whose "sartorial sense" matched his own, Marlon reported.

"Get to the point," Miranda said, but her smile evident in her voice.

As helpful as he was trying to be, James did not know of any good alternatives to the treatment option he had described to Jessica. He had hastened to add that ongoing research would surely result in more clinical trials for which Jessica might be eligible. But there was no guarantee, of course, and time's passage was not Jessica's friend, given her condition.

"On another note," Marlon continued, "I asked James if he knew your Dr. Glasser."

"Dr. Glasser?" Miranda asked. "The radiologist? Why?"

"Well, I just took a stab. Following up on what Renee told you this morning. They are both residents at the same hospital, after all."

"Hmm," Miranda, admiringly. "Smart thinking. And?"

"Said he's a total prick. Glasser was born with the proverbial silver spoon in his mouth and thinks he's god's gift to medicine. A back-stabber and wildly ambitious. James thinks Glasser would stomp on anyone who got in his way."

Miranda chuckled. "I guess James doesn't like the guy."

Marlon hooted. "You could say that," he said. "And just to be clear," he continued. "All that was on his own initiative. I didn't tell him anything about Renee. From what you said, she clearly didn't want her opinion to go any farther than the office. And listen to this," he continued, "Glasser had come to see James recently to ask how Jessica is doing. He had apparently looked it up and found out James is treating her. And," Marlon's voice deepened, "Glasser asked if Jessica had told James anything about her med mal case."

"How would Glasser ...?" Miranda began.

Seeing where she was going, Marlon cut her off. "Everyone at the hospital who had been involved in her care would know we'd gotten Jessica's records," he said.

"You're probably right," Miranda admitted. "So," she continued, "Glasser would like to know if he might be sued. Sure. But why do we care?"

"Think, Miranda," Marlon tutted. "Glasser would have easy access to a large, white rat. From the research labs. And the screws. Used in orthopedic surgery all the time."

"Ohhh," Miranda exhaled, getting it now. "You think?" she asked.

"Just could be," Marlon replied. "But I doubt we'll ever know for sure. From the sound of the guy, he sure wouldn't ever admit it."

•　　　•　　　•　　　•　　　•

Will powered down his Kindle, zipped the case and returned the device to its slot in his briefcase. He stood and walked, again, the few yards from his seat to the passageway leading out of Customs. He peered again down the thirty-yard stretch. Nobody. He looked at his watch. Thirty minutes since the last passenger had emerged into the International Arrivals Lounge. What in the world was going on?

He had gotten to Dulles Airport right at seven, parking in the expensive, close-in, short-term lot. Norma would be tired. Not from the flight, which was just over four hours from Mexico City. The hours sitting bedside at the hospital, listening attentively as the doctors gave their explanations and predictions, waiting anxiously for the nurse to arrive with the pain meds, begging the kitchen help for something the patient could actually eat, scheduling meetings with dieticians and therapists and social workers. As anyone who has cared for a loved one in the hospital with a serious illness knows, Will thought, it is grueling.

Norma had told him in yesterday's call. Her mother, home from the hospital, was doing well. Luckily, though the heart attack had been serious, it had caused little permanent damage to the heart muscle, according to her cardiologist. Norma hated to leave her so soon, but work was busy, and she was still fairly new on the job. She would email him her flight information later in the day.

Will arrived twenty minutes before the flight was due, which would land right on time as per the app on his phone. Given the time it would take for the passengers to deplane; board and disembark the squat, boxy shuttles from the gate to the main terminal, that feature of the Dulles terminal universally despised by passengers; and be processed through immigration and customs, he was well over an hour early.

But he liked it that way. Will had to travel a lot for work, flying to Cleveland or Miami or Denver, and to Sioux Falls and Kalamazoo and Wichita, mainly to interview witnesses. He chose to travel on vacation, to places farther away, and more exotic. Nonetheless, Will still felt a thrill of adventure whenever he stepped inside an airport, perhaps because he had not flown at all until his mid-twenties. He loved watching the planes take off and land and imagining what the well-dressed older woman planned to do when she landed in Berlin.

He also had two, unread novels on his Kindle. After one stroll down the concourse to the east end of the airport and back, he sat in an uncomfortable plastic chair in front of the information board in the Arrivals Lounge. He took out his Kindle and began one of his books, glancing up now and again to read the board.

Her plane landed at 6:40, on time. At 7:05, the entry beside Flight 2035 from Mexico City changed to "In Process." Four other flights were also reported as "In Process." Will hoped the immigration desks were well-staffed this evening. Norma had only carry-on luggage so she should sail through once she cleared immigration.

A few passengers had wandered out into the Arrivals Lounge while Will was reading, but by 7:30 they were emerging in droves. Will stood and joined the others lined up outside the last security barricade between those excitedly waiting and those joyously, if tiredly, arriving. He grinned, thinking of Norma's pleased smile when she caught her first glimpse of him, waving his arms high in the air to catch her attention in the crowd.

By the time forty minutes had passed, impatience and a hint of irritation had displaced Will's happy anticipation. If for some reason she had gotten off the plane before it took off, she would have let him know. What was she doing back there? Had she bumped into an acquaintance, and they were chatting away, oblivious to the passage of time? Not likely. She never took long in the bathroom. Or ... Will was suddenly worried. Maybe she fainted in the bathroom, hit her head on the sink basin and was lying there, knocked unconscious. Don't be ridiculous, he told himself. But still ...

He took one more look up the corridor then started walking in, towards customs. The place was deserted. He walked on, but when he got to the door between customs and immigration control, it was locked. He could not see clearly through the opaque glass walls. He pounded on the door. "I need help, please," he shouted.

The door sprang back. A uniformed man, ICE insignia prominently displayed on his chest, gun in his holster, stood in the door frame. "You're not allowed back here," he said tonelessly.

Will quickly explained.

"If she's been stopped for questioning ... And I mean if, because I can't tell you anything at this point. She'll be released when the interview is over. If she's to be detained an agent will call you, assuming she identifies you as the one to notify."

"What do you mean, detained?" Will asked.

"Put in a custodial facility," he agent answered.

"You mean jailed?"

"Well, it's an immigration detention facility. Not, technically, a jail. But her movements would be restricted. She would be under guard."

Alarmed and confused, Will asked, voice strained: "But what is this all about? She's got valid papers. She was only in Mexico a few days to visit her sick mother. I just don't understand."

"I don't have any answers for you, buddy," ICE agent responded dismissively, turning back, pulling the door closed.

Will spent the next hour trying, fruitlessly, he suspected, trying to find someone who could do something. Get answers from ICE. Get in to see Norma. Get Norma away from ICE. He was sure she would eventually be released from questioning, but how long might that take? And he had a sick feeling in his gut that if the authorities could hold her for questioning at the airport, they could put her under guard. He went to the airport security office. Closed. He talked to the only ticket agent he saw on this side of the concourse, at the United counter. Of course, she could not help. He reluctantly called Norma's father, hating to worry him but needing to know if he knew anything, anything at all about what was going on. He called the U.S. Attorney's office in the District and left a message on the answering machine. He called the office of the U.S. Representative from the District and begged the young intern answering the phone to relay his story to her as soon as possible.

His phone rang. "Will McCarty here."

"Mr. McCarty, this is agent Bruce Williams from Immigration Customs Enforcement. Your wife, Norma, is being transferred to the immigration detention facility in Chantilly, Virginia."

The agent hung up. Will quickly checked "recent calls" to re-dial. The last one recorded was his call to his Representative. Of the call from Williams, there was no record.

Chapter 15

Miranda walked into Jim's office at 9:00 a.m. "Where is everybody?" she asked. Saturday morning was a good time to get things done. Rarely were client meetings scheduled over the weekend, except right before trial, and the phones would be fairly quiet. Usually, most of the lawyers would be in early, researching and writing briefs, hoping to finish in time to have some time for r&r in the afternoon. But today, the office was strangely empty. "Aaron and Lauren left for Cleveland early this morning, but where are all the other lawyers?"

"Will called in sick," Jim answered.

"That's odd," Miranda observed. Jim nodded his head in agreement. Will was such a trooper. Miranda remembered the time Will was scheduled to defend a client's deposition. He had woken up with stomach flu. He came in, anyway. Will was the only one who knew the case, and he did not want to risk asking anyone else to defend it. A persuasive client depo was the keystone of a successful med mal case. As good as Aaron's lawyers were, they would be hard-pressed to do a top-notch job defending with an unfamiliar set of facts. Plus, it had taken forever to schedule this deposition because there were three defendants, and two of them had flown in from out of town for the depo. They would complain to the judge if Aaron's firm asked to re-schedule at the last minute. Will just excused himself a few times during the six-hour depo to go into the bathroom and barf. But he got the job done.

"Kim is in Philly for a depo and won't be back until late this afternoon," Jim continued. "Cassandra and Betsy are working in the Bar library today. Not sure why, but whatever. Marlon should be in any minute."

Miranda nodded. "Kathy and Jessica?" Once she had made her decision the evening before, Jessica wanted to get it over quickly, before she had a chance to change her mind. Kathy had been prepped to be prepared to conduct the hypnosis whenever Jessica was ready if her decision was a go. Kathy, who had rented a van equipped for a wheelchair, had stopped by Jessica's house earlier to pick her up.

"Aaron's office," Jim answered.

"That seems an unlikely place," Miranda objected. "Who could get relaxed in there?"

Jim laughed. "It's not bad so long as Aaron isn't in it," he said. "Besides, that's the only place that had room for that big lounger Kathy insisted we rent. And we lowered all the blinds. It's really quite nice. Go on back," he turned back to this computer screen. "They're expecting you."

Miranda and Jessica had had a long talk on the phone with Kathy last night, as Kathy walked Jessica through the procedure they would attempt the next day. Kathy started by telling them to forget everything they ever thought they knew about hypnosis. Kathy wasn't going to be waving a stopwatch or anything else in front of Jessica's eyes. Nor was she going to be putting Jessica into anything they might think of as a "trance."

Instead, Kathy had explained, she would be talking Jessica through a relaxation exercise intended to help Jessica into a meditative state. Someone who had been meditating religiously on her own for years, with the occasional meditation retreat along the way to deepen her skills, could probably do this on her own. But Jessica had not, so she would need some guidance. Then, when Kathy had done her best to help Jessica free her mind from ordinary thoughts, Kathy would ask a few carefully-phrased questions. If all went well, the lost memories they were seeking would re-appear, as it were, in Jessica's receptive mental tranquility.

Miranda opened the door and walked into Aaron's office. She smiled. Jessica looked relaxed, perched in a comfortable lounger instead of her usual wheelchair. She walked over, reached down and patted Jessica's hands, clasped together in front of her. "Are you doing okay, Jessica?" she asked.

"I'm okay," Jessica replied. "A little scared, sure. But," she turned and smiled at Kathy, "I'm in good hands. The best." It was Kathy's turn to smile. "And I can't imagine this could be nearly as bad as some of the stuff I've been through the last year, stuff I didn't choose," Jessica continued. "This is my choice."

"We're ready now," Kathy said, motioning for Miranda to leave. "I'll come by your office when we're finished."

"Or you could call me in here when you're done," Miranda suggested. "Maybe Jessica shouldn't be alone so soon after."

"She won't be alone," Kathy replied. "I've brought my nurse, Roseanne, along. She's waiting in the large conference room. She'll monitor Jessica while we're talking, and then we'll take Jessica to Georgetown."

"The hospital? Why? Are you expecting ...?" Miranda cut herself off abruptly and glanced at Jessica.

"No, no," Kathy said impatiently. "I've gone over all the possible complications with Jessica, of course, but nothing bad is likely to happen. I just want to be sure. I want to have her monitored for twenty-four hours, in a place where I could provide treatment immediately. If necessary. I checked her in for a routine neurological evaluation," Kathy grimaced. "Not exactly kosher, but I sure as hell wasn't going to put 'post-hypnosis' as the admitting diagnosis."

Miranda smiled to herself. Kathy was a unique bird. Barely five feet tall, lean and wiry, Kathy was born in the mountains deep in West Virginia sixty years ago, her father a coal miner. She had somehow managed to get into medical school at a time when few women were admitted. And then she had succeeded in a specialty practically reserved for men. Kathy was only the third female pediatric neurologist in the country to be board certified. The tales she told of the treatment she got from her male colleagues were hair-raising. She had scrabbled together a good practice, even though the male GP's were reluctant to refer their patients to her. A woman. She was just too talented, though, and she made it. Kathy had had to be tough as nails, though, and it showed. Not with her patients, though. They loved her.

"Will you go with Kathy and me to the hospital, Miranda? Roseanne is lovely, but ..." Jessica trailed off.

"Of course," Miranda said firmly. She stood up and, looking directly at Jessica, smiled broadly. "See you in a few," she said and left the room.

• • • • •

"In five hundred yards, turn left," intoned the GPS lady, as Will thought of the familiar, disembodied voice coming from the dashboard. Thank goodness for satellites, Will thought. He had never been in this part of Alexandria before. He had visited friends who lived out here when all of them were young lawyers needing the less expensive housing the Virginia suburbs offered. Will still came out to the Old Town area for dinner or a concert now and again. But he had never had the occasion to come to or even pass through Alexandria's old downtown, with its squat, down-at-the-heels office buildings populated with bankers and lawyers and accountants in an earlier era. Most of them had decamped to one of the more prosperous suburbs, or one of the D.C. areas newly-gentrified by the expanded Green Line of the Metro. The lawyer Will was scheduled to meet at 9:30 a.m. still had her office here.

What he had really wanted to do yesterday evening, after losing his wife in the maws of immigration authorities, was to hit somebody or something, to express his fear and anger and frustration. But no. Justice would be done, he was sure. But he needed to play his part in it. To follow the right procedures. So, he walked out to his car, started home, and began a series of calls. He needed an immigration lawyer. Not just someone would do. This was going to require a lot more than knowing which form to fill out to apply for an F-1 visa. And it would have to be some immigration law superstar with an opening in his calendar – tomorrow – for another client.

Which was possible only in a town like DC. It had scads of lawyers, for one thing, though the bigger metropolises like New York and Chicago certainly had more. In DC, however, the lawyers all knew each other, too. Young lawyers flocked to DC to begin their careers working in one of the dozens of Federal government agencies. Some stayed, some left for private practice. The private law firms' clients had business with government agencies. Returning to the Department of Justice, or the FBI, or the IRS to represent those clients, their attorneys found themselves across the conference table from their former colleagues in that agency. Hill staffers took lobbying jobs, in which positions they returned to the Hill to ask favors of their former bosses. Lawyers left firms to work in think tanks, in which they prepared position papers to send out to lobbyists and their old partners in the firm. Marlon joked that in DC, lawyers are not linked by "six degrees of separation" but by one.

Critics argued that DC's "revolving door" corrupted government agencies. If you are a young lawyer at the SEC, you do not accuse a Wall

Street firm of illegal insider trading if you have your eye on that firm for your next job. But for those in the network, it was the richest source for a precious commodity: trusted referrals to the person with the exact credentials needed for any job.

A friend, if a regular opponent, as well, in the defense bar recommended that Will call Marla Tuckman. "She's ferocious," he had said, "and smart as a whip. She's talented enough to be litigating for any big firm in the city, making a ton of money. But she's devoted to her clients, many indigent. Admirable. Not for me," he hastened to add. "But I do admire her." And he had her cell number.

"Arriving at destination." Somehow the GPS lady always sounded satisfied when she said that, Will thought.

Will pushed open the lobby door of the nondescript, four-story building. He confirmed the office number she had given him last evening on the directory plaque posted on the left wall of the smallish lobby, behind the deserted receptionist's desk. Suite 101, down the corridor to the left, according to the numbered arrows on the wall in front of him.

Will knocked. The door was opened by an older woman, maybe in her sixties, Will guessed, wearing a silky cream blouse and navy pants suit. She was a couple of inches taller than Will's five foot eight even in the navy flats she was wearing, with a sturdy, fit-looking build. She smiled and held out her hand: "Marla Tuckman. You're right on time. Come on in."

She motioned him to the straight-back, wooden chair in front of her desk, which was Marlon-style, Will thought: Only a small pile of documents stacked neatly next to her open laptop lay on it. The office was small but neat. Business-like. He saw no family pictures or other personal items.

Will had briefed her on the phone the night before. Now she wanted details. He told her the whole story, as he knew it. "But it just doesn't make any sense. She has a valid visa. I sometimes get a question or two from immigration when I return from another country, but they questioned her forever. What could they possibly have been asking about, all that time?

"You'd be surprised how often that happens. How often non-citizens, even those with valid entry documents, are stopped and questioned at the border," Marla answered. "There are no rules, here, at least none I've even been able to identify. They can ask about anything and everything, or nothing. I've had clients who sat in a little, windowless room off the main immigration processing center for hours. Now and again, an ICE or INS agent would come in and ask a few random questions, then leave. I suppose one in a thousand times the questioning produces some evidence of a crime being committed or having been committed. Even something serious like running drugs. The vast majority of these stops are just annoying and humiliating, however. But routine."

"Is it also routine to take them away to some detention facility like they did Norma?" Will asked.

"Definitely not," Marla stated firmly. "ICE may well deserve its reputation for barging into factories and fields, willy-nilly, and hauling out unsuspecting undocumented workers. But even ICE has to have a reason to put a documented person into a detention facility."

"Such as?"

"If there were probable cause to believe a crime had been committed, of course, the person can be detained," Marla responded. "You told me on the phone it was impossible Norma had committed a crime or had been involved in anything criminal. For now, I'm going to assume that's true. The other common reason for an initial detention is some defect in the entry document. Her H-1 visa, in this case."

Will shook his head. "This makes no sense to me, either. Her employer, Mid-American, sponsored her visa. It's a big, international energy company, and they do this all the time. They have employees from all over the world, going to other countries to recruit the specialists they can't find here. Or they can't hire as many as they need. As you know, the industry is booming, and it's hard to find good people. Norma's education and experience are top-notch. I can't believe her documents aren't in order."

"Speaking of documents, you did apply for her permanent residency, didn't you?" Marla asked.

"Yes, of course," Will responded. "Less than a month after we were married. But you know how it is these days. Even something that should be so simple and straightforward takes forever."

Marla did know. Before 9/11, she had been able to complete the process for getting citizenship and passports for clients newly-married to American citizens in weeks. INS turned its attention to other matters when the Towers came down, and couples waited longer. With the current administration's new, "zero tolerance" crack-down on illegal immigration, matters got even worse. Processing legal immigrants was by far the agency's last priority.

"Listen, Will, this situation may have nothing to do with Norma, personally," Marla said. "She might fit some fact pattern that raises suspicion or casts doubt on the documents whether there is, in fact, a problem or not."

"What do you mean," Will asked.

"Let me give you an example," Marla said. As I'm sure you know, a person born in the United States is a citizen of this country and entitled to a U.S. passport. About a decade ago, some investigator discovered that a birth certificate provided by a person of Mexican descent, living in Texas, who was applying for her U.S. passport, had been falsified. The midwife who prepared it affirmed that the birth had taken place in a hospital in south Texas. In fact, the person had been born in Mexico. So, no U.S. passport for this person."

She sighed, leaned back into her chair, and continued. "The problem was, the State Department then started denying the passport application of anyone of Mexican descent who was delivered by a midwife. That was absurd, of course. They were unfairly assuming that all midwives in Texas regularly forged birth certificates, although, in fact, they had no evidence of this at all. Just the one isolated forgery was ever proven."

"How do you know all this?" Will asked.

"I was part of the team of lawyers headed by the ACLU who sued State. We got a settlement agreement. State agreed to stop this practice. And they re-processed the hundreds of people in the class action whose passport applications had already been denied. Every one of them eventually qualified for and got their U.S. passports."

"And in the meantime? I mean, before everything was straightened out, were those people treated as legal or illegal immigrants?" Will asked. "Because if Norma's been caught up in something like that, it's going to take a while to figure it out, of course. What's going to happen to her in the meantime?"

"In our case, nothing changed after the passport applications were denied. All of the applicants were already living in the States, and they just went on with their ordinary lives until the case was resolved."

"Whew, that's a huge relief," Will smiled broadly.

"Not so fast," Marla shook her head. "It's a crime to knowingly make a false statement in connection with immigration proceedings. If it had been true that the birth certificates were forged, State would have deported those people unless they could prove they had no knowledge of the forgery. Nothing happened in our case because the judge issued an injunction shortly after we filed the case. The government was under court order not to take any action against the plaintiff class until the case was decided."

Will stood suddenly, placed both hands on the desk, and leaned over towards Marla. "I heard you wrong, or you misspoke. Innocent until proven guilty in this country, right? But I thought you said they'd have been deported unless they proved their innocence."

"You heard right. Welcome to the upside-down world of immigration law."

Will fell, abruptly, heavily, back into his chair. He was quiet for a moment. Then he looked straight at Marla and said, in a disbelieving tone: "We don't know which 'statement' they are concerned about. Norma submitted dozens of documents to her employer and the INS to get her visa. Nor do we know what was allegedly false about that statement. How in the world would you prove you were innocent of something when you don't even know what that 'something' is?"

"You're right. Worse than upside-down. Kafka-esque," Marla said, her voice flat. "The first thing to do is for me to get in to see her," she continued. "I'll start making calls."

"Call me as soon as you know the time. I'll meet you there," Will said.

Marla sighed. "No guarantee you'll get to see her, Will. One lawyer is usually all that's allowed. As I said, Will, a different world."

●   ●   ●   ●   ●

Miranda glanced at her watch. Almost 11:00. They had started at about 9:30, and Kathy had predicted it would take about an hour. Should be soon, now. Miranda wondered for the hundredth time whether anything would come of this. At least Kathy had not come flying out of the conference room, shouting for someone to call an ambulance. Something caught her eye, and she looked up. Nor Kathy, though. Marlon was leaning on the doorjamb of her office.

"Nothing yet, I presume," Marlon said.

"No, but it should be soon now," Miranda confirmed. "Come on in."

Just then, Kathy appeared at Miranda's office door. She looked tired, face more drawn than usual, Miranda thought, but calm. "Everything is okay," Kathy said. "Jessica seems fine. No adverse reactions, at least not yet."

Miranda breathed a heavy sigh of relief. "Well, and, did she remember anything?"

"Yep. Here's ..." Kathy was interrupted by her phone. She looked down at the number, answered, and listened for a couple of minutes. She then turned and, tilting the receiver away from her lips, whispered, "have to take this." She walked away.

"Doctors," Miranda huffed. "Always waiting on them." Marlon chuckled. Like other professionals accustomed to stressful working conditions, uncertain outcomes, and the need to take risks, the lawyers could still laugh though worried and anxious about the outcome of the hypnosis. As with surgeons, who crack jokes over the operating table, humor kept them human.

Kathy walked into the office a few minutes later. She got right to it. "She did have recall. Actually, quite detailed. And as far as I can tell it's real. You can be sure I didn't plant it, at least."

Kathy quickly told the story Jessica remembered under hypnosis. Jessica had taken an Uber out to the NSA facilities and called another one after her meeting with Paul to take her home. She waited and waited at the main gate. No Uber. She had thought the lot would be well-guarded but, surprisingly, there was no one in the gate's guard booth. Jessica called Paul, but he did not answer the ring, and there was no way she would be allowed back into the building after hours unless he escorted her. Jessica tried Uber again just as her phone died. She was about to walk around the enormous campus to see if she could find a guarded booth when a man approached her, keys in hand. She asked where he was going, and he said into the city. Jessica explained how she had been stranded, and he said he would give her a ride. She figured she would be safe because he must work for the NSA. As he was backing out of his slot, he rear-ended a car in the next row. It wasn't so much a crash as a bump, but Jessica's head did snap back onto the headrest. She remembers driving towards D.C. but doesn't remember getting home."

"That's it?" Miranda asked.

"That's it."

"What's the guy's name?"

Kathy looked chagrined. "Unfortunately, that's one of the details she doesn't remember," she answered

"So how does this even help us?" Miranda groaned.

"Well, what did the guy look like?" Marlon asked.

"She doesn't remember," Kathy responded. "Just a guy. Who looked normal."

"What's 'normal' supposed to mean?" Miranda asked.

"I don't know. That's Jessica's word. Nothing she can specifically describe other than that he looked ... 'normal.'"

"Great, so what can we do with that?" Miranda asked.

"I don't know, but now's not the time to figure it out." Kathy stood. "Let's get Jessica to the hospital."

Kathy drove the van to the hospital. Jessica was quiet and pale, Miranda had thought as they rolled her chair up the ramp to the van and did not say much. But otherwise, she appeared unscathed by her recent experience.

Kathy pulled up under the porte cochere of the main entrance. She and Miranda hopped out to get Jessica. "Wait just inside," Kathy instructed. I'll park and be right back."

As Kathy drove off, Jessica wheeled herself towards the doors, Miranda right behind her. As they approached, the automatic doors opened. The inside doors opened at the same time, revealing a man exiting the hospital. "The bike guy," Miranda cried. He stopped in the passageway momentarily. "What a coincidence! I guess you did hurt your hand, huh."

Suddenly, Jessica cried out, loud and shrill. She started to shake violently in her chair. "Oh, god, no, a seizure," Miranda wailed, dropping to her knees in front of the wheelchair. Kathy had warned them that though unlikely, the hypnosis could trigger a seizure or other temporary neurological disturbance. Jessica was sobbing hard, hands in her face. Her whole body quaked. "Jessica, Jessica, oh dear, where's Kathy?" Miranda was close to tears, herself.

"I'm here," Kathy said calmly as she grabbed the handles of Jessica's chair and pushed her quickly into the hospital.

Miranda looked around quickly before she ran after Kathy and Jessica. The guy had disappeared.

Chapter 16

1995

The boys had breezed through high school, getting A's with little difficulty. MIT was different. They studied late into the night.

They had no time for nor need to use any of their "sources and methods," the phrase from the spy novels Ed had devoured during high school that they now used instead of the chess plays that ever only loosely described their special maneuvers. When they found an hour of free time together, however, they did add to their tactical oeuvre, at least conceptually. They also discussed their plans for after college.

Chad was going to Silicon Valley. He had made a name for himself in computer software. Ed was going to Wall Street, where there was an increasing demand for "quants," mathematicians and applied statistics grads to put hard science to pricing and risk analysis. Chad was aiming for fame. Ed, for fortune.

•   •   •   •   •

Chad loaded his last box in the back of his father's Chevy. His parents had driven up from Fort Hood, where his father was now stationed, for the graduation. Chad closed the door and leaned into the open, passenger side window. "I'll be back in a minute," he said. His mother nodded.

Chad hurried back to Killian Court, where many of the graduates and their families were still lingering. Ed's step-father, Jay, had run into an old acquaintance, and Jay had been making introductions when Chad and his family left. Chad figured they might still be there. He had one last thing to say to Ed.

Chad trotted up, nodded to the group, and pulled Ed aside. "Be good," Chad said, nodding firmly.

Ed grinned broadly. "Do well, Chad," he said.

The two shook hands and parted. It would be four years before they saw each other again. For the first couple of years, they talked often over the phone, however, keeping up with each other's successes and failures.

Chad had a job lined up before he left for California, having scored at his number-one choice among software development companies, located in Berkeley. Chad quickly found a reasonably-priced condo in Albany, very near Berkeley. He was close enough to walk to work, though he often hopped on the BART to get home after he left the office late at night.

Chad loved the Bay Area. And though he was working hard, and very long hours, he was learning fast and meeting lots of other very smart and ambitious people in the industry. Things were looking promising, except Chad worried about Ed.

Ed did not get straight to Wall Street. For months, he did not even get an interview. For a while, he thought he was going to have to change his career path. A lot. He tried his hand at a few other jobs, and even went back to graduate school for a year. But then, Ed's fortunes seemed to turn. He found a mentor, a "super-smart, super-talented professor," as Ed had described Dr. Wilson to Chad. Dr. Wilson hired Ed as his graduate assistant for the spring term, and then helped Ed land a great summer job.

And then it all fell apart. Again. Ed called Chad and complained bitterly. Chad commiserated. Before they started the argument.

"Jay was right about the recurring bad luck, and it's your damn fault I didn't do anything to stop it," Ed concluded his story, angrily.

"Now wait, just a minute," Chad began, but Ed cut him off.

"It might be too late, but this time we need to do something about it," Ed commanded. "Hit back, hard."

Chad told Ed his reaction was stupid and superstitious. These things had nothing to do with luck, good or bad. Chad had to admit, though, that this time, the consequences had been life-altering. Ed had lost his job, and, it looked like, a career. Not like the last time when Ed just lost his place on the football squad.

"Screw you," Ed was shouting now. "I lost Coach. That lying punk led Coach to believe I was a terrible sport and a bad person. Coach couldn't even look me in the eye when he told me I was off the team."

That shut Chad up. For a few minutes, he just listened to Ed's heavy breathing, thinking hard.

"Ed, listen," Chad finally broke the silence, "I'm sure it was an honest mistake on their part. They were just trying to do the right ..."

"I don't care," Ed's shout interrupted him.

They yelled at each other for a while, calming down eventually to the level of a heated argument. Finally, they both fell silent. Chad sighed.

"Look, you'd need my help, anyway," Chad said, "and I really don't have the time right now. Not a spare minute." Chad had told Ed in an earlier conversation that he had found a "terrific" partner, brought in a few more people, and launched his software development business. Not any revenue, yet, but great prospects. "You can always come out here, you know," Chad continued. "There will always be a place for you in my company."

"Nah," Ed said, "not for me. Thanks, though, buddy. Heh," Ed continued, "that reminds me. Jay said you should be thinking about an asset protection trust agreement with your partner, or whatever other legal instrument a good lawyer recommends."

"What's that mean, and what's it for?" Chad asked.

"I don't know, exactly," Ed replied. "But something to make sure everything stays on the up and up with the business. Jay said to tell you the rule is not 'trust, but verify.' It's 'don't trust.'"

Three months later, Ed called, elated. He had gotten his big chance. His job trading on Wall Street.

•   •   •   •   •

A year and a half later, early evening, Chad poured another two fingers of the cheap whiskey into his shot glass. He glanced around at his dark, one-room apartment, furnished with a thinly-sheeted mattress on the floor and a small wooden table and the one chair in which he sat, and downed the drink.

He had relocated to this apartment building in a run-down section of Oakland, hard by the bus station, with its small, rusty window panes laced with security bars and a scattering of broken windows on the upper floors of its five stories because it was what he could afford. And because he had never run into one of his former colleagues in this part of town. Or anyone else he knew.

Chad started hard, tipping his plastic chair sideways when he heard the knock on the door. "Go away," he called out immediately, in the roughened voice, stained with cigarettes and booze, that still surprised him.

"It's me, Ed," Chad heard clearly through the battered panels of the wooden door, the charcoal-colored varnish of which was peeling off in ragged strips. "Open the damn door."

They had not talked in over a year, and as he rose, Chad wondered for a brief second how Ed had found him. At that thought, Chad almost grinned. Of course. Ed had his sources and methods.

Ed made Chad change into a semi-clean shirt before they left the apartment. Chad had not been to it in a while, but there was a decent diner down the street, Chad had said.

It did not take long to catch up on the basics. Later, they would re-hash the details ad nauseam.

Ed had been making a little "adjustment" in brokering a massive short sale, a ploy that could have netted Ed half a million in one fell swoop when he was caught by his supervisor. They all did it, Ed explained to Chad. That is how they all got so rich, so fast. And none of the buyers or sellers was really hurt. They simply did not get exactly what they had hoped from the transaction. The supervisor had said he would let Ed off with a warning. Neither he nor the other brokers truly cared if Ed cheated. So long as nobody caught him doing it. Ed had, instead, been made to look the fool. It was time to go.

Chad had made a major breakthrough in a technical problem that had bedeviled the entire industry. Just as he had found a lawyer he trusted and was on the verge of filing for a patent, his partner, in very public fashion, accused Chad of stealing the idea from him. The partner, already a well-established developer with patents of his own, and with a sterling reputation, was believed over the relatively unknown upstart. Supposedly he had real evidence to support his claim, too, although Chad did not believe it. Because the idea had been entirely his own. He had stolen not a bit nor a byte.

Ed made the appropriate noises of dismay and anger and disappointment on hearing Chad's story. Asked the right questions. "Are you sure nothing can be done?" "Have you consulted a lawyer?"

And then Ed sat back in the booth and laced his fingers behind his head. "Sucks, doesn't it?" he asked, a hint of smugness in his voice.

As he had listened to Ed, Chad sat quietly, saying nothing, eyes cast down, fiddling with his coffee cup. He told his story in a monotone. But now he looked up with fire in his eyes.

"This time, it's completely clear," Chad said, voice shaking. "He lied to ruin and steal from me. He'd do it again if he could get away with it. He's the foe, pure and simple. It's World War II." Chad pounded his fist on the table between them, breathing hard. After a few minutes, he asked: "Are you in?"

"Of course, I'm in," Ed answered quickly. "I'll help you get the bastard," he continued. Then Ed held up both hands, palms out. "But with conditions."

They talked until midnight when the diner closed. As they were walking out the door, headed to the nearby hotel the proprietor had recommended because Ed had decided there was no way Chad was staying in that dump one more night, Ed said he knew how they would start the game.

"I'll bite," Chad said. "What've you got in mind?"

"Industrial espionage," Ed intoned. "In this," he continued, "we will be superstars."

Chapter 17

Just after noon on Saturday, Miranda walked out of the hospital and headed for the cabs waiting patiently in line at the bottom of the hill. "Dupont Circle, Connecticut and Q, please," she told the cabbie as she slid into the back seat. She took her phone out of her bag and rang her lunch date. "Heh, Sully, I'm on my way. Might be a little late, though."

"No problem, Miranda. I'm still trying to find parking, anyway. See you in a few."

Miranda put in her next call right after Sully hung up. "Heh, Marlon, Miranda. We had a problem at Georgetown." She explained what had happened.

"Oh, no," Marlon sounded uncharacteristically anxious. "Is Jessica going to be all right? What's Kathy say? Oh, this is awful."

"Hold on, Marlon," Miranda soothed. "Kathy examined her and found no indication of a seizure or any other neurological explanation of her sudden breakdown. Kathy thinks it was an emotional reaction. Not from the hypnosis, exactly. Jessica has been under a lot of stress for a long time, anyway, and in the last few hours that was compounded by fear and anxiety about the procedure, and about what she might remember. I don't think she slept at all last night. Tough stuff."

"So, what now? Are you still at the hospital?" Marlon asked.

"No, Kathy said I might as well go. Kathy will stay with Jessica, as she was planning to do, anyway. She gave Jessica a mild sedative, and Jessica will sleep until late this afternoon, probably. Kathy will call one of us when Jessica is awake and report, but she expects Jessica will be fine. Tired, but fine. No follow-up on the parking lot incident at the NSA, though, until tomorrow. At the earliest. Doctor's orders."

"I'll update Aaron," Marlon said. "Are you on the way back to the office?"

"No, I'm meeting Sully for lunch. He called me right after I left Jessica's room, on my way out of the hospital. Said we should meet asap. He doesn't say much on the phone, but he said it's about Paul. Aaron would want me to follow up on anything having to do with Paul, for sure."

"Of course," Marlon agreed. "See you back at the office later." Marlon hung up.

The cab stopped at the light at the intersection of Connecticut and Q Street. "Where do you want out?" the cabbie asked.

"This is fine," Miranda said. She handed the cabbie a twenty, said "thanks, keep the change," and climbed out, slamming the door just as the light changed and the cab drove on. She walked east on Q towards her favorite restaurant in Dupont Circle, Thaiphoon. The restaurant was crowded, but she spotted Sully at a booth near the back of the place.

"So, what's this about?" Miranda asked as she slid onto the bench across from Sully. She had brought Sully up to date on everything that was going on at the office when he had called with the contact information for Deren. Sully must have something useful for the problems she was trying to solve if he had called her up here on such short notice.

Sully started to answer, then paused as a waiter approached and handed out menus. "We're ready to order," Sully said quickly before the waiter could turn away.

"How do you know I'm ready?" Miranda protested.

"Why waste time? You always get the same thing," Sully responded. "Pad thai, right?" he continued.

Miranda nodded. "Yep. Stuck in a rut," she said sheepishly.

"And drunken noodles for me, please," Sully waved off the waiter. "I want to examine Paul's computers, Miranda, assuming the investigators imaged them and allowed Paul to retain possession. Do you know?" he asked.

"I'm pretty sure Paul's still got them. His lawyer does, anyway. Because Aaron mentioned that they'd hired a computer expert to see if he could find anything. Something that would exonerate Paul, or at least show something fishy about the investigators' search for evidence that would justify a Fourth Amendment motion to suppress. Do you want to look at them, too?"

"Yeah, I do," Sully answered.

"Because you're better than he, whoever he is? Or think you are," Miranda smiled at her friend.

"Well, I probably am better," Sully said, a note of pride in his voice. "But this time, it's because I know more than he does."

"Explain," Miranda said.

"Months ago, when I examined Deren's work computer ..."

Miranda interrupted. "You were part of the NSA's investigation of the data breach? The breach supposedly executed by Deren?"

"Well, yeah, that's my job, silly. You know I do cybersecurity. Digital forensics, specifically. I look for evidence of what happens when data is accessed. The who, when, and how."

"I know, Sully," Miranda said. "Sort of," she amended quickly, "but when you were so sure Deren was telling the truth, and that he didn't do it, it seemed to me someone at the NSA missed something or planted something, maybe, I don't know. Something like that to explain it all. But if you were in on the investigation of your friend, that didn't happen."

"You're right, Miranda. I looked under every rock, so to speak. And I did find something."

The waiter brought their food. "Well, what was it?" Miranda demanded after the waiter had deposited their plates and turned away.

"I found a fragment of anti-forensics code in the address space of a program running an intrusion detection analysis ..."

Miranda interrupted by pointing the fork she had intended to stab into her noodles at Sully. "Forget the jargon, Sully. I can't understand it. Dumb it down for me."

Sully smiled. "The theory in the industry is that a hacker always leaves a clue. The evidence can be hard to find, but it's always there. I'm not so sure about that, myself, but I did think I'd found the footprint of a stranger. Something that shouldn't have been there. Faint, and indistinct, but something."

"Why didn't you say anything before?" Miranda asked, surprised. "When you told me Deren had to be innocent?" Miranda looked down and speared some noodles. "That surely would have clinched it," she said as she popped the forkful into her mouth.

Sully shrugged. "It's the investigator in me. I need to be sure about something before I rely on it. Or ask someone else to rely on it."

"In other words, don't presume," Miranda said primly.

Sully looked a little surprised. "Yes, right," he said. "Anyway, the other members of the investigatory team weren't convinced. They thought the bit of code I found was just an artifact, accidentally left behind by a legitimate program."

"Of course," Miranda said, "I get it. Because they did fire Deren, after all."

"Ah," Miranda grinned. "I got this, too. You'll look for the same footprint on Paul's computer. If you do, it will confirm that you found something suspicious after all."

It was Sully's turn to grin. "Not so dumb after all, Miranda!"

Miranda pulled her phone out of her bag after she had swatted Sully's on the wrist for that one. "I'll call Aaron right now. He'll contact Paul's lawyer. Could you look at the computers soon, if we can make it happen? We don't have much time. Until this coming Thursday, at the latest. They moved the expected date of the indictment up once. They could do it again."

Sully agreed. Miranda made the call. They quickly finished their lunch, paid, and left.

• • • • •

Later that afternoon, Will slid into the driver's seat of his Prius, closed the door, strapped on his seat belt. He pushed the console button, and the hybrid engine noiselessly ignited. He checked his GPS, then started towards Chantilly. The traffic would be brutal at this time of day, but he should arrive before 5:00. He had no idea if that made any difference, but he would get there during "normal" office hours. As though this was an office, he thought sourly.

Marla had told him the facility in Chantilly wasn't what he was probably imagining and fearing from seeing the news about the detention of immigrants on the Texas border with Mexico. Detainees from Dulles were usually housed in an old Holiday Inn the government had condemned and then converted to function as a suspect traveler processing center. Norma would not be able to leave the facility, and she would not be allowed to communicate with anyone outside. But she would have a room and bath, and meals would be served to her in her room.

Will arrived at the address Marla had given him at just about four-thirty. It was unmistakably an old hotel. He could even make out the shadow of an "H" logo that had been scraped off the portico over the glass-fronted main entrance. The building needed a new coat of paint, but it looked sound enough. Will saw no broken windows, at least.

The entrance doors still opened automatically when Will approached, but from there, the resemblance to a hotel ended. The inner door, into what would have been the lobby, was now a solid, windowless wall. In the center, chest high, hung a telephone receiver. Will lifted the receiver off its bracket and, holding it to his ear, heard it ringing. "Chantilly Center," said a male voice.

After fifteen minutes of arguing with the agent, explaining to the supervisor to whom the agent reluctantly transferred the call, then yelling mindlessly when the supervisor disconnected, he left. No authorized appointment, no visit. He was assured his wife was perfectly safe and comfortable and that her case would be promptly processed.

Will was not at all assured. But Norma had Marla. This would all take time to sort out. He had to believe, as per the old saying, that though the wheels of justice grind slowly, they grind exceedingly finely. Norma was innocent, and she would be sent home. Will looked at his watch. No sense going back to the office this late. After a few moments of indecision, Will started the car. He would do what he did best. He did not know much about immigration law yet. But he soon would. He drove home, booted up his laptop, and started researching.

A couple of hours later, Will's phone rang. He looked at his watch. Eight o'clock. It was Marla's number. He had a million questions for her, starting with the bond hearing. He assumed Marla had already put in a request for one, and he wanted to be sure they were prepared.

"Hi, Marla," he answered. "How's Norma? They presumably took her phone away at the airport, but she should have been given the opportunity to use a phone at the facility to make her one call. Why didn't she call me? Did you find out why they are holding her? She'll be released on bond, right? When is the hearing?"

"Okay, okay, hold on," Marla interrupted. "Just let me talk for a minute. Questions to follow. Since Norma was delivered to the facility by ICE, she's been shepherded around by a series of female guards. They are in uniform but have so far been pleasant and courteous. But she is under guard. She looks fine. She's clean and well-dressed, and she confirmed she has a room with a bathroom en suite and that she's being fed. Not great food, but edible. She was terribly anxious when I first met her, but she eventually calmed down."

"Of course, she was anxious. But why didn't she call me?" Will repeated.

"One of the guards told her the landline was out of order."

"That's absurd," Will said angrily.

"Remember, another world. I was only able to interview Norma. Which means we won't have any idea why she's been detained until the bond hearing. Before we get to posting bond for her release, I'll object to her detention. The attorney from State will have to provide evidence showing probable cause, given that Norma does have the visa. If the detainee has no documents, State doesn't have to have other evidence to justify the detention."

"So, when's the hearing?" Will asked.

"Monday afternoon. The court convenes at 2:00."

"Why so late in the day?" Will's voice rose. "Can they really hold her that long without giving us a chance to post bail?"

"I assume you mean 'can' from the legal point of view. The answer is, unfortunately, yes. The immigration court is justifying the delay on the grounds that they don't have the resources. Hundreds of immigration judges were transferred down to the Texas border recently because of an influx of immigrants from Guatemala and El Salvador. They are short-staffed here and doing the best they can."

Will sighed, loudly, into the receiver. "I know you're angry and frustrated," Marla responded, "but I've seen a lot worse. I've seen a four-year-old immigrant child, alone and crying, no idea what's going on, behind bars. Norma is not in a jail. She knows she'll be out in a couple of days and that we'll all clear all this up. She's a big girl, Will."

"She's also my wife," Will said. He sighed again, less vehemently. "I've been doing research. I doubt if you need it, but I wanted to have a better handle on the process. And it gave me something to do this afternoon. Is there anything specific I can help with between now and Monday? Research or otherwise?"

"I can't think of anything, Will, but thanks." They made arrangements for meeting at the immigration court, then Marla rang off.

Will rose from his desk and walked into the kitchen. He thought about coffee for a minute, then thought, what the heck. He opened the kitchen door and pulled out a bottle of Corona. He sipped, standing at the counter, gazing out the living room windows into the dark evening.

It was in his first year of law school when a different conception of his parents' differing world views occurred to Will. Professor Ferguson was relating the historical divide between law and equity. As the common law system developed in England in the middle ages, law courts heard cases involving disputes over title to land and what payment was owed the farmer by the miller for a cartload of wheat. Over time, the judges' decisions in individual cases were woven into rules regarding property and contracts, and those rules – now the common law – were followed in subsequent cases. A separate court of equity would decide whether a couple was lawfully married and whether an apprenticeship should be terminated early because of the master's incompetence. Gradually the divide between law and equity virtually disappeared, although courts in the United States still, on occasion, looked to equitable principles in making its rulings.

Professor Ferguson concluded the lecture: "The law is justice as defined by applying the same rules derived from sound reasoning to all equally. Equity is fairness, as determined by individual circumstances." And that summed up his parents just about right, Will had thought. His mother was law, his father equity. His mother was all about following the rules. His father thought it right and necessary to flout authority on occasion.

Although Marla's words about this being another world were still ringing in his ears, Will did trust the justice system. It had never disappointed him. It surely would find that Norma was innocent. But what if it did not ... And how the hell was he supposed to get through Sunday?

●   ●   ●   ●   ●   ●

Sunday evening, Chad got out of his car, slowly, and raised both hands high in the air as the agent approached. He would be searched. Not for guns, he knew. Nobody in his situation would carry a gun. He would not be stupid enough to be wired, either. No, the agent would be looking for any device that could be tracked by GPS or any other location identifier. No one would know what was said at this meeting, and no one would know there was a meeting at all.

Search completed, Schwartz appeared out of the gloom and waved off the search party. Chad supposed there were other agents in the area, but all he could see were the faint outlines of trees surrounding the grassy opening in which he stood. He could barely hear the susurration of moving water, the Potomac River off to his right.

Schwartz stopped about a yard from Chad. Close enough to talk softly, but not too intimate. Schwartz, broad shoulders slightly hunched, feet braced widely, arms akimbo looked ready for a fight. If necessary. Chad reached across the space between them, gingerly, a small, black mesh bag in his hand. Schwartz took it, pulled the drawstring enclosing the bag, and looked inside. Schwartz grunted. He unzipped his jacket and stuffed the bag into its inner pocket.

"We're about ready to pull the trigger," Schwartz then said, tone soft but gruff. "I assume one of my guys talked to you about the money?" he asked.

Chad shook his head, no. "They talked to me, all right, but I don't want your money."

"Why, then?" Schwartz asked. "I don't really care," he quickly added, "but I confess to being just a little curious. He was your partner. Still is, as far as he knows. Right?" Schwartz added, a trace of anxiety in his voice.

Chad nodded firmly. "It's a long story," Chad said, dismissively. "I think we're done here," he then said, and he turned and walked into the darkness.

Chapter 18

Monday morning at 7:45, Marlon walked into the offices of the Internal Medicine Group. The chairs in the waiting room were empty of patients, but the receptionist was stationed at her desk. Marlon approached, introduced himself, and was ushered down the hallway off the lobby into a small conference room. The first to arrive, Marlon took a seat, swung his briefcase up onto the table, unlatched it, and pulled out his Kindle.

Miranda had asked Marlon to cover this deposition, which had been on Miranda's calendar for weeks, so she could get to the hospital to see Jessica Monday morning. Kathy had called Saturday afternoon, while Miranda was de-briefing the lawyers on her meeting with Sully, and told them in no uncertain terms that nobody was to disturb Jessica until Kathy gave the all-clear. Jessica was in too fragile a state. Kathy herself needed to deal with her other patients, as well as Jessica, and nobody was to bother either of them until Kathy let them know otherwise. Miranda passed the depo to Marlon just in case. Luckily, for Kathy had called late Sunday evening to tell Miranda she could come to see Jessica early the next morning.

Marlon lowered his Kindle when an older woman in a loose, black cardigan, long gray hair tied back in a braid, walked into the conference room. "Hi, Grace, good to see you again," Marlon smiled at the court reporter. She smiled back, said, "hello, Marlon," then took a seat at the end of the conference room table. They made small talk as Grace pulled her recording mask and digital recorder out of the large, black leather case she had sat at her feet, and positioned her equipment neatly on the table in front of her.

Many attorneys ignored the court reporters, as they were called whether they were employees of the court preparing the written record of everything said in the trial or worked for private reporting companies engaged by the many law firms and government agencies in town to record proceedings in law-making and law enforcement functions. To these busy lawyers, court reporters were just necessary cogs in the litigation machine. Other attorneys were courteous, but not interested in getting chummy with the "help."

Marlon had a different approach. He believed the court reporter could be a real asset. For one thing, the reporter was the first person without a vested interest in the case to hear the evidence. In a way, a proto-juror. If the court reporter liked one of Marlon's key witnesses and believed her testimony, that was a good sign. If not, maybe he had better think about settling the case. He could also ask the reporter, after a deposition was over, whether any of the testimony was fatally confusing. That problem Marlon could fix, but it was better to be aware of it before the trial. The reporter would not likely be forthcoming about such things if she were treated like a machine, though. So, Marlon took pains to be friendly with the reporter who showed up at his depos. Besides, he had found, the reporters were usually just interesting characters.

Aaron's firm used two or three different reporting companies, each had a goodly roster of reporters, and reporters changed jobs or moved out of Washington. Sometimes Marlon would walk into a depo and find a reporter he had never seen before. But others, like Grace, had been around forever and stayed with the same company, and Marlon had gotten to know her quite well over the years. He knew the kinds of books Grace read and the names of her grandchildren. They had also gotten into the habit of discussing each other's cases. Those Marlon was litigating, and those Grace was recording.

After they had chatted a bit, Marlon asked: "Cover any interesting cases recently, Grace?"

"One just last Friday," she replied. "High-profile, too," sounding just a bit smug.

Grace explained that a lawyer representing one of the detainees at Guantanamo Bay deposed a representative from the Department of Defense. The detainee had filed a lawsuit against the DOD, claiming that it was violating Department of Justice policies and other laws protecting freedom of religion. The DOJ policies required all federal agencies, including prison administrators, to safeguard the right to practice one's religion. As Grace understood it from the questions and answers, the detainee's lawyer was arguing that if convicted felons had the right to practice their religion, the Guantanamo detainees should, too.

"Fat chance, I'd say," Marlon said when Grace finished her story. "I'm not saying I agree with it, but those prisoners are just not going to be given anything except maybe deportation to Afghanistan or Syria."

"I don't know for sure," Grace responded quickly, as they heard people, presumably the doctor and his lawyers, coming down the hallway toward the conference room. "But this administration is seriously pro-religion. And from the witness' answers, I'd say they might just have a case."

●　　　●　　　●　　　●　　　●

At about the same time Marlon started the depo, Miranda walked into Georgetown Hospital. She checked at the reception desk to confirm that Jessica was still in the same room. She took the elevator to the neurology unit on the seventh floor. The door to Room 705 was open. Miranda stepped in and smiled. Jessica was awake, sitting up in her wheelchair, reading the front section of the Washington Post. Kathy sat, eyes closed, in the bedside chair.

"Hi, Jessica, how are you feeling?" Miranda asked softly, approaching Jessica.

Both women looked up and smiled.

"Okay," Jessica said. "Actually, much better today." She set the newspaper aside.

"Do you still remember what you remembered?" Miranda asked, then chuckled. "Well, that's not quite right. I'm not sure how to put it."

Kathy spoke up. "Jessica doesn't remember anything about the hypnosis or about talking to me during the session. But she has recovered the actual memory of what happened that night. It's the same now as she described it to me during the hypnosis."

"So, we know, or think we know what happened to Jessica, but not who did it. Just a normal looking guy is all we have," Miranda said, frustration in her voice.

Jessica's smile disappeared abruptly. "I'm doing the best I can," she said, voice trembling.

"I know, Jessica," Miranda said quickly. "I'm sorry. I didn't mean to upset you. It's just ..." she paused. "I don't know what else we can do."

"And there is something else," Jessica's voice had firmed. "Kathy, will you explain it?"

Kathy nodded as she stood up to stretch, explaining as she did so that she did not think Jessica's breakdown was caused by the hypnosis. Instead, it was caused by shock. The shock of encountering that man who was leaving the hospital as Jessica and Miranda were entering.

"You mean the bike guy?" Miranda asked. At Kathy's puzzled look, Miranda quickly explained their encounter on the towpath.

"Oh, my," Kathy said, a rare note of delighted surprise in her voice. "I'm pretty sure your 'bike guy' must have been the driver of the car," Kathy continued. "The guy who was giving Jessica a lift back into town after her meeting with Deren. Jessica can't consciously remember what he looked like. But her unconscious mind does. Then she comes face-to-face with the actual person, right after she'd dredged up his memory from her unconscious mind, and bang. Sent her over the edge."

"Ha!" Miranda whooped. "Incredible coincidence, but so now we know not only what happened to Jessica, but who did it. We may have a case," she said triumphantly.

"So, you did get his name?" Kathy asked.

Miranda's face immediately fell. "No. I don't know who he is," Miranda said. "Damn it," she groaned. "I don't know anything about him." She sighed. "I'll go back to the office after we get Jessica discharged. Maybe someone else will have an idea."

•　　•　　•　　•　　•

Later Monday morning, Jim stood in front of the mirror in the small dressing room, arms bent behind him, struggling at the small of his back with the cummerbund fastener. Cheap, Jim thought, but then what else could you expect of the low-rent tuxedos the caterer provided his staff. "Heh, Roberta, can you fix my cummerbund, please?" he asked of the young woman to his left dressed in a short, black dress, sheer black hose and shiny black heels, also in front of the mirror, pulling her hair up into a tail.

"Sure," she responded. "Turn this way."

Jim was trying to save up enough to buy a condo, he hoped in the Logan Circle area. His salary at the firm was quite generous, above-market, certainly, for a scheduler-cum-client-hand-holder. But DC real estate was extremely pricey, and at the beginning of the summer, Jim started looking for a part-time gig to supplement his income. When he asked Marlon for ideas, Marlon had suggested he try for a waitstaff position with a catering company. It paid better than other jobs in the foodservice industry, he had said, and if Jim could land a position at one of the high-end caterers, the hourly wage would be higher than most other unskilled jobs.

"These people getting paid big bucks to serve the glitterati in this town want good-looking waiters. Brains enough to learn how to serve the soup. But it's the brawn that matters."

Jim, at six-foot-two, two-hundred forty pounds, ripped from hours at the gym, blond, blue-eyed, square-jawed, could have played an extra in a movie featuring Vikings plundering Greenland. A gay Viking, though. His sexual orientation was obvious when you talked to Jim. Phil Penelton, owner of Food for Thought, a prominent, Georgetown-based caterer, could not have cared less. And he had a fix just in case some of his clients did care. Jim did not need to open his mouth to serve. He was a handsome hunk who looked terrific in a tux, and that is what mattered.

The event this noon was in the Old Executive Office Building. The former name of the old belle, Jim knew, which he clung to fondly even though the building was not officially designated the Eisenhower Executive Office Building. The hulking behemoth of a building, its French Empire architecture contrasting sharply with the neo-classical facades lining Pennsylvania Avenue, housed White House staffers and other officials of the administration. In a private meeting room on the top floor, Jim and Roberta carefully placed china and silver and crystal on the white linen cloth covering the room's large, rectangular table. The staff was rarely told much about the people they served, or the reason for their meeting, and today was no exception. But given the locale, Jim presumed he would be serving government people and, given the choice of caterer, probably some big money people, too. Government contractors, lobbyists, and their lawyers. Mostly if not all men, too, Jim predicted.

Table set, Jim and Roberta returned to the adjoining kitchenette, where Penelton and his sous chefs were buzzing around finalizing the food preparation. Penelton barked instructions to Jim, Roberta, and two other waitstaff Jim had not met before, and the serving began.

Later, as the other Food for Thought staff cleaned the kitchenette and packed up the remnants of the luncheon, Jim and Roberta cleared the dining table. As usual, they quipped about the people they had just fed. Exchanging catty remarks about the guests eased the humiliation of being totally ignored by them during the meal.

"I didn't recognize any of them," Roberta said. "But I'd say deputy assistant secretaries, at best, from the look of their suits," she continued.

Jim laughed. He reached down to retrieve a wine glass. "Except for that guy sitting here. He buys at Saks. Or better. I think his suit was bespoke. And, man, was he drop-dead good looking. A hottie." Jim pantomimed fanning his face with his hand.

It was Roberta's turn to laugh. "Out of your league, dear," she said. "I overheard some of the conversation during dinner. That guy is a bigwig in cybersecurity. The name of his company caught my attention. Cerberus."

"Why'd you notice that?" Jim asked, scooping the last of the china plates onto the pile he was holding.

"Cerberus is the three-headed dog guarding the gates of hell in Greek mythology," Roberta replied. "It struck me as an odd choice for a data security firm. Who'd want to hack into hell? Anyway, we're done here. Let's go grab a drink."

•　　•　　•　　•

As Jim's lunch gig was ending, just before 2:00, Miranda arrived back in the office, much later than she had hoped. But Kathy had had to leave to see another patient, and Miranda wanted to see Jessica safely home. With all the baton passing from doctor to nurse to social worker to van driver, the discharge itself had taken forever.

Miranda gave a passing hello to Cassandra and Betsy as she walked down the corridor past their offices, then walked in to see Marlon. He looked up as she entered his office. "Is everything okay at the hospital? You look worried," he said.

Miranda brought him up to date. "I feel terrible," she concluded. "We may have had a case for Jessica. But I didn't think to ask the guy's name."

"If you can get your friend Sully to help, the problem may be solved," Marlon said.

"What do you mean?" Miranda asked.

"Think, Miranda. We've been imagining a person hacking the NSA and Jessica somehow getting in the way. But now we know it was just a fender bender. So now it seems more likely that the culprit was just an ordinary NSA employee leaving for the day."

"So, why do we care about him now?" Miranda sounded confused. "We wanted him as the hacker."

"Remember, the surgeon who operated on her said the hematoma could have been caused by minor trauma. Probably was caused by a minor trauma, in fact, given that no other cause was detected. Jessica hit her head when the guy collided with the car behind them. There's your case. Simple negligence causing massive damage. Unfortunately for both of them."

"Yep, you're right," Miranda said, musingly. "And if I describe the guy to Sully, he may be able to tell me who he is. I wouldn't think that would violate any protocol."

"Might work," Marlon said. "It's an awful big agency, though. And with agents stationed overseas most of the time whom Sully might never have seen. But you've told me Sully's very smart. Maybe he can come up with some other way to identify him," Marlon continued.

Miranda nodded slowly. "Hah," she suddenly cried. "I know another way. A better way. DNA matching."

"What are you going to match with what?" Cassandra asked.

"I presume the NSA keeps its employees' DNA on file. And I've got blood from the bike guy. Smeared all over a sweatshirt stuffed in my laundry basket."

Marlon, who knew about the bike incident but not the bloodstained sweatshirt, looked nonplussed, for once. Momentarily. "Okay, then," he said, "let's call someone who knows something about DNA typing and get going."

Marlon had stepped out of the office to get a cup of decent coffee just before 5:00. When he returned, walking through the main door to the office suite, he heard Beebee say, "as soon as you can, Cassandra. And call Kim and tell her to come in, too, okay?"

"What's going on?" Marlon asked.

"Everybody's to come in, and we're setting up a war room," she answered. Marlon looked puzzled. He knew what a war room was, of course. That was what they turned the large conference room into on the eve of starting a trial. The chairs would be pulled away from the table and lined up against the walls. The bankers' boxes containing all the documents collected or produced during the evidence-collecting phase of the litigation would be retrieved from the file room and emptied onto the table. Whiteboards would be set up on easels to be used to chart witness lists and staff assignments. Anatomical models or diagrams or enlarged photographs, whatever would be used to explain the case to the jury, would be perched on easels or tables or chairs. A desktop and several laptops would be brought in, plugged in, and fired up.

"But we don't have a trial coming up," Marlon said.

"It's worse than that. Will called Aaron a few minutes ago. Norma is being deported. Aaron told me to call everyone in. Will needs our help. Right now."

"What?" Marlon asked, shrilly. "Deported? Why in the world would they deport Will's wife? That's crazy!"

"Yep," Beebee said, "it sure is." Her phone rang. "Go on into the war room," she said as she reached for the receiver. "Aaron will tell you what's going on."

•   •   •   •   •

Twenty minutes later, all the lawyers except Kim, who was on her way, waited in the war room for Will. Miranda, sitting by the conference room table in front of a glowing laptop, asked the room at large: "Any idea what we're going to do?"

"Let's hear the whole story from Will. He should be here any minute. Then we'll brainstorm," Aaron responded.

Will strode into the conference room, where all the other lawyers were gathered, a little after five-thirty. His suit was rumpled, his eyes were reddened, and as everyone spoke at once, he sat down abruptly and put his face in his hands.

Aaron's voice rose above the din. "Start from the beginning, Will."

Will told them what had happened since Friday evening. "I'm scared, guys. Very scared. Norma never showed up at the bond hearing. Marla said this might be just some bureaucratic screw-up, and ICE will dump Norma at one of the processing stations south of the border, and we'll start working on getting her back. But Marla doesn't know whether she'll be allowed to see Norma again, because we don't know what went awry. And…" Will paused, clenched his fists, and took a deep breath. "What if Norma did do something wrong? Something illegal? And she ends up in jail? With all due respect to Mexico, the story on the street is that once someone lands in a Mexican jail, all bets are off. I don't want to lose her. I do love her, even if …" He stopped abruptly.

Everybody sat silently for a few minutes.

Marlon broke the silence. "Why didn't you tell us before, Will?" he asked. "When she was first detained?" he continued.

"I don't know. I just ..." He paused for a moment. "None of you know anything about immigration law. I got her the best lawyer I could find. I was sure she would be out on bond today, and it would turn out this was all a terrible mistake. I never suspected it could go so wrong. And I don't think any of you particularly approved of my marrying her. It was so sudden and all ..." Will closed his eyes and heaved a deep sob.

"Humbug," Marlon said, but gently, and he squatted down beside Will, putting his hand on Will's shoulder. "You should have known better. But now you're here. In the right place. And I have an idea," Marlon said.

"You do?" Will asked, dubious, but with a faint note of hope.

"Tell," Aaron commanded.

"We need to find a liberation theologist," Marlon answered.

"A what?" Miranda asked.

"A priest," Marlon answered.

Chapter 19

2004

Chad and Ed had had a good ride with industrial espionage. They had honed old and acquired useful new skills for their upcoming ventures. Made some money, too, to Ed's great satisfaction. Ed thought they were ready to move on. They took several months to lay the foundation for their pivot to a slightly different venture. The keystone would be the new program Chad had coded.

They had agreed not to go with a high-priced patent attorney. Instead, they would go with someone low-rent, who would not ask too many questions or demand too much background information. Besides, Chad's nemesis would presumably be on the look-out, and they did not want to have the name of one of the well-known patent firms on the application. And once they had the program up and running, Chad had opined, they would be ready to take him out. The men, out on Ed's catamaran on the Chesapeake Bay on a sparkling Saturday afternoon in June, discussed their plans.

"It would be too soon," Ed complained as he hauled on the jib line as the breeze freshened. "I'm not sure we could manage even a check, let alone mate. He could easily escape. And we could be exposed. Too risky," he concluded.

Chad reached into the cooler, pulled out a can, and popped the tab off a beer. "Yeah," he said, stopping to take a swig, "but it's also risky if we wait too long. It may become impossible to do the switch. He'll be too powerful for us."

Ed shrugged. "That's a different kind of risk," he said. "I'm prepared to take that one."

"You may be, but I'm not," Chad said, an undertone of anger in his voice.

"Look, buddy," Ed drawled languidly. They had talked about it often enough. He knew Chad's anger would quickly dissipate. Chad always managed to address the hard issues with clear-eyed dispassion. "We're doing this together, and we're doing it the right way. When everything is lined up. No matter how long it takes."

Chad laughed. "Are you done with your speech?" he asked. Ed quickly bent down, grabbed an empty can from the trash bucket, and pitched it at Chad, laughing. Chad deftly caught the can in mid-air.

"The right way," Chad said, musingly. "I guess," he continued. "Although we don't have to take out your targets in order to capture mine. Any other pieces on the board could work just as well."

"Get over it, Chad," Ed said, his turn to reach into the cooler and grab a can. "That's the deal. Besides, they're only temporarily taken. Not out of the game completely, like yours. That's what makes it right."

Chad leaned back against the mast and closed his eyes, basking in the sun. "Fine," he said, without opening his eyes. "You've convinced me. For now." After a few moments, he sat back upright. "By the way," he said, "who're you going to be now? The old version or the new?"

Ed grinned. "Haven't decided yet," he answered. "Maybe somebody entirely new. But," Ed stood, unopened beer clenched firmly in his uplifted left hand, flexing his arm, "always still me, old buddy."

Chad laughed. "What do you do about that, anyway?" Chad asked.

"Ahh, no big deal," Ed answered. "Say," he continued, "it's got to be mid-afternoon, and I'm starved. Come on, let's sail back into Annapolis and get some lunch."

Chapter 20

"It's already 5:30," Aaron said, "and we have no idea when Norma might be taken. And all we have so far is this ridiculous idea of a priest. What's a priest going to do?" Aaron's voice dripped sarcasm. "Perform a miracle and spirit Norma out of jail somehow? Does anybody," Aaron looked out at his assembled team, "have a legitimate idea?"

A particular kind of priest, Aaron," Marlon said. "Let me explain."

Marlon told the group about his morning's conversation with the court reporter. "If we can find the right priest, maybe, just maybe they'd let him in to see her before they put her on a plane. And by the right priest, I mean someone who believes civil disobedience in the face of unjust laws is an appropriate way to work towards social justice. I should say believed, because the Church put a stop to that wing of the clergy that was prominent in South America in the '60s and '70s, fighting against despotism and corruption on behalf of the poor."

"How do you know all this?" Cassandra asked.

"I read," Marlon replied tartly.

Will broke in abruptly. "What good would that do?" he asked. Will stood up and paced across the room, then turned back. "We need to get her out, Marlon!" practically shouting. "Before she's taken out of the country."

"At least we might find out what's going on," Marlon protested. "Why they canceled the bond hearing," he continued. "Why they've decided to deport her. Whether this is just a huge paperwork headache for us or ..." Uncharacteristically, Marlon failed to finish his sentence.

"Or," Will's voice, low and rough, picked up where Marlon had left off, "she's done something wrong, and we send a priest to hear her confession? What kind of crap are you talking, Marlon? Damn it anyway," Will pounded his fist on the conference room table.

Marlon did not blink. "No, no such thing, Will," he said. "The priest would simply tell the guards he was hearing her confession. That's the pretext to get in to see her. He'd really be there to find out what was going on. That's why we need a special kind of priest."

"Why do you think the authorities would have told her anything?" Cassandra asked.

"I just don't believe the government would fly Norma back to Mexico without giving her any reason why," Marlon answered. "I may be wrong. But it wouldn't hurt to find out. But we need someone who can get in to see her, and you said Marla might not be permitted, Will. So, does anybody have a better idea?"

"Let's find out," Aaron said. "But we've got other balls in the air, too, and we've got to keep an eye on all of them. And that's why," Aaron stood up, briefly surveilling his team, "I ordered the war room." In the next few minutes, he gave them their orders. Marlon and Cassandra would work with Will on the priest project and anything else they could think of to help on that front. Miranda's job was to keep on top of Sully's investigation of Paul's computer and follow-up quickly on the DNA tracking. Kim would review the lawyers' regular case calendars and do whatever needed to be done to clear everyone's schedule for the next day or two. Aaron would check in with Paul and keep in touch with everyone. "Get to work," he concluded.

An hour later, Will rang the doorbell of a four-story row house on the far eastern reaches of the Capitol Hill area. As he waited, he noticed the fainted paint of the façade and the spreading crack in the step on which he stood. He knew that the floors of the building above Justice for Immigrants' first-floor offices served as a home for retired priests. They were fortunate to have a home, he supposed. Few if any priests could afford to save money for retirement. But the parish sponsoring this one certainly wasn't spending a lot of money on their aging clergy.

The door opened, and a tall, thin man in a black shirt and pants, white collar around his neck, stepped out. With his deeply-lined face, pronounced stoop, and bald head splotched with irregular brown discolorations, he looked to be around eighty years old.

Will had not been to Mass in years, but he had been raised Catholic. "Good evening, father," Will said, bowing his head slightly.

"You must be Will," the priest responded in a strong baritone that belied his aged appearance. The priest reached out with both hands and clasped one of Will's. "I'm Father Brennan. Come in, my son," he said.

The priest motioned for Will to follow him through the vestibule and into a long, rectangular room that must have been the living room in the original row house. Now it held rows of office desks, each covered with its unique array of phone, papers, magazines, coffee mug, writing pads and pens, and the occasional flower vase. Father Brennan led Will towards the rear of the room where an old burgundy sofa with sagging cushions sat against the wall.

"Our conference room," Father Brennan said with a smile. "Make yourself comfortable. Can I get you something to drink? Coffee or water?" the priest asked Will.

"No, thank you, father. What have you decided?" Will blurted.

Will had explained about Norma on the phone. The priest had not said no outright. But he was clearly dubious. Yes, he had given communion to detainees and heard confessions. But this was different. Was Norma even Catholic, he had asked? Assured that she was, he said he would think about it and agreed to meet right away.

Father Brennan sighed. "I doubt if the Bishop would approve. But I don't think I'd be doing anything wrong. Not breaking any laws, that is. I will truthfully be asking to see her in order to give her communion. And hear her confession, if she so desires. I'll also ask her if she knows anything about why she's being deported, of course. That raises something I wonder if you've thought about, Will. What if she does confess, and she confesses to a sin?"

Will flushed. "What do you mean?" he asked the priest.

"I can't tell you what she says during confession, of course, but what if I come back and tell you she's being deported for a good reason? Are you prepared for that?"

Will suddenly clenched both fists and, looking down, blurted: "I've thought of that. I don't think it's possible. I think the authorities made a mistake if they think there is a good reason. Maybe. I don't know ..." Will trailed off. "One way or another," he continued, "I need to know."

●   ●   ●   ●   ●

Miranda glanced at her watch. Almost 8:30 in the evening. She picked up her pace. Sully would wait for her, but she did not want to keep him waiting long. She entered the park, choosing the diagonal path. She passed the statue of Andrew Jackson on his rearing war horse in the center of the park and walked quickly on to the southeast corner, where she was to meet Sully by the park's eponymous statute, that of the Marquis de Lafayette. As Miranda neared Pennsylvania Avenue, she caught sight of his tall figure.

"Hi, Sully," Miranda said, reaching up to give him a quick hug. "Did you find anything?"

"I did. Come on, let's walk. I've been sitting in front of Paul's computers for hours." They started down the wide pedestrian walkway past the White House. Commuters hated it when this block of Pennsylvania Avenue was closed to vehicular traffic after 9/11 for security's sake. But the resulting promenade gave tourists a wide berth from which to ogle and take pictures of the lovely façade of the President's residence, so serene in the evening light. Only on the outside, Miranda thought.

"Well?" Miranda asked a few minutes later, impatiently.

"I detected a footprint," Sully responded. "I understand why Paul's expert missed it, though," he continued. "it's very faint. You'd pretty much have to have seen the one on Deren's computer to find it. And," he shook his head, "unfortunately, it's not quite a perfect match to the one on Deren's."

"So, what does that mean?" Miranda asked.

"I believe it's the same intruder. One left foot, one right, let's say, but the same person. I'm not sure I could convince anyone else, though."

"So, what do we do now?" Miranda asked.

"I don't know for sure. I'm still processing," Sully replied. "By the way, why are you working so late? What's going on?"

Miranda brought him up to speed.

"Did I guess right that the NSA has DNA samples of its employees?" she asked.

Sully nodded affirmatively. "And I bet you want me to check our DNA database and identify your bike guy, right?" he asked.

Miranda beamed. "You got it," she said excitedly.

"Not going to happen," Sully said firmly.

Miranda paused and turned toward Sully, catching his arm. "But Sully? You said you'd help if you could. This is a big deal, you know. If we can identify this driver, we save Jessica's life. How could you ..." She stopped herself. It was not right to push him, she thought. To ask him to compromise his integrity.

Sully reached across his chest and disengaged Miranda's hand from his arm. "I said I'd help if I could do so without violating my responsibilities as an NSA employee. I can't access the DNA database to find a defendant for you to sue. That is not a proper purpose."

"I ..." Miranda sighed. "I understand," she continued.

"But ..." Sully began. Something in his voice made Miranda look up at him sharply.

"There's a but?" she said, hopefully.

"I will check to see if the man was an NSA employee."

"You lost me," Miranda shook her head. "Why's that okay? And why would you do it?"

"I'm trying to clear Deren, remember?" Sully answered. "I'm also just doing my job," he continued. "NSA was hacked. They think it was Deren. I don't. So, it's my job to find the actual culprit and do what I can to prevent it from happening again. As soon as possible."

"But," Miranda said, shaking her head, "if the DNA matches an NSA employee, that just means he was the guy who picked Jessica up in the parking lot on his way home from work. That fact alone doesn't mean he had anything to do with the hacking. So, how does running the DNA for a match help to identify the hacker?" she asked.

"It won't if the DNA matches an employee," Sully said. "But I don't think it will."

"Because?" Miranda asked.

"I tend to trust my colleagues. Which means I'm presuming the hacker wasn't supposed to be on the premises. I haven't found any evidence of that yet, though. I've checked the visitor logs, and, other than Jessica, nobody except employees should have been in the parking lot that night. The DNA from the shirt would confirm that we did have a physical intruder. And that fact would substantiate my digital intruder theory."

"Hmmm ..." Miranda mumbled. "Something's missing here ..." she paused. "Oh," startled. "It all keeps coming back to Jessica, doesn't it?" she continued. "Because that all works only if you believe Jessica's hypnotic memory, which is that she and the source of that blood were both at NSA the night of the hacking. Otherwise, the blood and the DNA just match a guy who tumbled off his bike on the canal path."

"I know, I know," Sully said, impatiently. "We'll cross that bridge when we get to it. I'm just following the only lead I've got."

"Fair enough," Miranda conceded. "We should have the DNA analysis from the shirt at about 10:00."

"Tonight?" Sully asked, surprised.

Miranda explained. After her chat with Marlon earlier that afternoon, before anyone in the office knew about the Norma emergency, she had gone home, retrieved the soiled black sweatshirt from her clothes hamper, and brought it back to the office in a plastic bag. In the meantime, Marlon called a friend who had worked as an Assistant United States Attorney in DC for years. His friend identified a state-of-the-art lab that offered a three-hour max turnaround for the right type of specimen. The blood from the shirt should fit the bill. The lab's expedited services were only available to law enforcement authorities, ordinarily. Some arms were twisted, favors called in, and Jim hand-carried the sweatshirt to the lab, which had promised a quick analysis.

Sully nodded. "Good work. I'll cross-check the profile from your house, if that's okay with you, Miranda," he said.

It was her turn to look surprised. "Well, sure, but can you do that? I mean, I certainly don't have a secure network. It can probably be accessed by my neighbor, in fact. And what's your hurry?"

Sully smiled. "I keep telling you that you need to beef up your security, silly girl," he said. His smile disappeared. "I'd rather not do this in my office. I've cleared it with my conscience, but still ..." He trailed off. "I'm doing it for my friend, Deren, yes. But I'm also just doing my job. Which, as you well know, is protecting the NSA's data. If, as I suspect, some unknown person was able to access the NSA premises undetected and hack Deren's computer, we need to find him asap. Before he or one of his associates strikes again. And don't worry," he smiled again, "I've got a very secure VPN on my laptop to access our DNA database. I will not get anywhere near your network," he said firmly.

"Fine," Miranda said. "You can come any time. I'm going home."

"Okay," Sully said. "I'll run home and say hi to my girls first. I'll plan on being at your house at around 9:30. Call me if anything comes up before then."

"Will do," Miranda replied. "And tell Karen hi for me, Sully."

As Sully walked out, shutting the door behind him, Miranda thought back to the war room, where she had stopped after she brought the shirt to the office. Will, haggard and pale, eyes inflamed, paced up and down. He barely glanced at Miranda as he passed her. In his fingers, she spied an unlit cigarette. Will had not smoked in years. The others were still parked at their computers, yellow legal pads covered with notes and numbers strewn at their feet. Miranda had asked if there was anything she could do. Marlon looked hard at her and said they could only hope that the priest would be able to get in to see Norma yet that evening and call. Soon. She understood. They had not made any progress. She would just go home and meet Sully.

•　　•　　•　　•　　•

Miranda put down her book and jumped up quickly when she heard the knock. Miranda hastened to the front door and let Sully in. They exchanged brief greetings, then he followed her into the kitchen.

"How are your girls?" she asked.

"Beautiful," Sully said, grinning.

Miranda smiled. "Of course, they are," she said. "No results yet," she continued, "so I'm going to have a drink while we wait." Turning away to reach for the refrigerator door, she asked: "A glass for you?"

"None for me, thanks," Sully said.

The two settled into chairs at the kitchen table. Miranda took a sip of her wine.

"So, straighten me out about hackers, Sully," she said. "I imaged a computer nerd turned thief, staring at a computer screen in a darkened room, planning a data heist, or whatever," she continued. "But the hacker I know, or at least the guy we think is a hacker, just seemed so normal." She laughed. "On a bike, after all. A middle-aged man, peddling down the path on a beautiful afternoon. He seemed nice enough, too."

It was Sully's turn to laugh.

"They are just like every other profession in the world," he said. "They have conferences in Caesar's Palace in Las Vegas with keynotes speakers and workshops. Talking about their latest and coolest illegal exploit instead of the newest in medical technology. But the same idea."

"Huh," Miranda said. "I had no idea. Have you, by chance, been to one of these conferences?" she asked.

"Sure," Sully replied. "I've been to Def Con a couple of times. Def Con is an annual conference that's been going on for decades. Attracts hackers of all ages from all over the world."

"But aren't they afraid of getting caught at one of these conferences?" Miranda asked. "I mean, hacking is illegal, isn't it?"

"Yes and no," Sully answered as he reached out for the bottle nestled in a mottled, gray-and-white marble wine cooler on the table and topped off Miranda's glass. "'Hacking' is a loose term for a wide assortment of activities. What you're thinking of, I presume, is someone illegally accessing a database or network and stealing data. On the other end of the spectrum is a security software provider with a contract to detect software vulnerabilities in its client's databases or networks. How does it go about doing that? Hacking the client's data. And getting paid to do it."

"Huh," Miranda said, thoughtful. "I guess there's a lot of this kind of stuff going on, too, right?" she continued. "The big data breaches, like Equifax, where some 130 million customer records were exposed. And the political stuff, like the Russians, supposedly hacking into the Democratic National Committee according to the national security agencies."

Sully nodded. "More than you know. It's a huge problem," he said. "Look at it this way," he said. "I haven't looked into it for a while, but last time I did, a good estimate was that, worldwide, private businesses alone are spending over a trillion dollars a year to protect their data. It's not working. One in five will have their data hacked. "

"How can that be?" Miranda asked, incredulous.

Sully shrugged. "It's complicated. Let's just say data is meaningless without software. Software is complex, constantly changing, and vulnerable to attack. And the attackers are good."

"Why do it, though?" Miranda asked.

Sully laughed. "Are you kidding? There's huge money in stolen data. One set of thieves made hundreds of millions of dollars from customer data stolen from JPMorgan."

"How did they make so much money?" Miranda asked.

"Churned fake stock sales," Sully replied. "Those thieves were caught, though, because they kept their hands-on and used the data themselves. Most thieves sell it."

"And where in the world would you sell stolen data?" Miranda asked.

"On the black market. It's on the Dark Web. Well-organized, too. Some even have a return policy. Buyers receive a refund if the credit card information they purchased is no longer active because the owner canceled the card."

"Wow," Miranda marveled, "a regular business. An industry, even."

"Industries, to be exact," Sully said. "A really skilled dark hat hacker, meaning a hacker who steals data, might decide to put on a white hat. Patent the process for stealing the data and set up a legitimate company. Sell data security services. On the open market."

"That happens?" Miranda asked, picking up her wine glass, draining it.

"All the time," Sully nodded. "At least that's what we think."

"A patent," Miranda said, musing. "Patent," she repeated. "Something just rang a bell, but I can't quite ..." She stopped.

She suddenly jumped up from the table, knocking the edge. Her wine glass teetered.

"I knew he looked familiar," she cried.

"Who looked familiar?" Sully asked. "What are you talking about?"

"The bike guy," Miranda said, excitedly. "When I saw him on the bike path, I thought so, but I couldn't place him. He said he didn't know me. And he might not remember."

"Remember what?" Sully asked.

"I filed a patent application for him."

"You what?" Sully asked, incredulous.

Chapter 21

Miranda explained. "Years ago, I worked for a while with this group of lawyers doing pro bono patent work. Filing patent applications for budding entrepreneurs with no money. Or at least people who claimed not to have any money. My group was organized and sponsored by the U.S. Patent and Trademark Office. I filed an application for the bike guy. I only met him once, though. And it was a long time ago. That's why it took me so long to place him. But it's him."

"Sounds crazy," Sully protested. "Like you're cosmically tied to the guy or something. The patent, the bike crash, the hospital ..."

Miranda interrupted him. "DC is actually a small town, you know," she said. "Ten miles square, remember."

Sully smiled. Yes, he remembered from law school the Constitution's provision for this small slice to be carved out along the Potomac River, to be the site for the new nation's capital.

"Anyway," Miranda continued, "crazy it may sound, but it's true. I swear. And I remember drafting that particular patent application, too. Because I only did one like it. And it was a really tough application to write. I quit after that if I remember correctly."

"What was it?" Sully asked. "That is, for what invention did you file the patent?"

"Some kind of data access program," Miranda responded. "I kid you not," she said at Sully's surprised look.

"How could you even begin to write an application like that?" Sully asked. "You have to fully understand a program to get the examiners at the USPTO to approve the application and issue a patent. What do you know about programming?"

"Nothing, anymore," Miranda replied. "But I did take a couple of programming classes in college. Back then, I knew enough about the field to prepare the application. I couldn't do it today."

"Was the patent granted?" Sully asked.

"Yep. And I can retrieve it from the patent database. I don't remember my client's name, but I was on the application as the attorney of record."

"Pull it up," Sully instructed. "Let's put a name to your bike guy."

Just then, the doorbell rang. "Must be someone from the office with the lab report," Miranda said as she stood and walked to the front door of her house. They had decided to retrieve the report manually to forestall any delays at the lab in getting it faxed or emailed.

"Hi, Jim," Sully heard Miranda say. "Come on in."

Sully walked into the front room from the kitchen. Miranda introduced the two men. Jim handed Miranda an envelope and said he had better get back to the office. Miranda handed the envelope to Sully, who immediately excused himself and went back into the kitchen.

"You must be tired," Miranda said to Jim. "A full day at the office, and it's now what, 9:45? What do they need you for?" she asked.

"Hand-holding," Jim responded. "Aaron said everyone should stay around and look busy, at least. Will's about to burst at the seams. If the priest doesn't call soon, he's liable to jump over the White House fence in a fruitless attempt to get to the President. Or some other crazy thing."

"I'm staying here for now," Miranda said. She explained what was going on and told Jim to relay the information to Aaron.

"Got it," said Jim. "Good luck, players," he waved and walked out.

We sure need it, Miranda thought. Luck that is. She checked on Sully, who was glued to his laptop screen. "How long will you take?" she asked him.

He looked up briefly, then returned to his screen. "Not long. The database is constructed for a quick cross-check. Maybe fifteen minutes."

"I'll be in my office. Looking at patents," Miranda turned and left Sully at the kitchen table.

Twenty minutes later, Miranda called Marlon. Down at the office, they were still waiting for the priest to call. Miranda told Marlon her news. The bike guy was not an NSA employee. Not just a guy giving Jessica a ride on his way home from work. He must be the hacker.

"I liked him better as an employee for Jessica's case," she complained to Marlon. "A nice government worker with good insurance, no doubt to sue for negligence. But this sure works for Deren and Paul."

She then reported that Sully was out in his car, making a call to his boss, Steve Schwartz. Sully was confident he now had enough evidence. He had his two footprints from Deren and Paul's computers, and an unauthorized presence at the NSA at the time of the data breach, if you believed Jessica's hypnosis-induced memory. The facts were shored up by the patent for a data access program by the intruder.

"You lost me there. What's that about a patent?" Marlon asked.

Miranda explained about her pro bono work. And while Sully was checking the DNA, Miranda had found the application and the bike guy's name on it. A Joe Smith, if that was his real name. And far too common for a google search to be of any help in finding him now.

"But NSA will find him. Sully's sure they will re-open the data breach investigation now.

"There's surely another possibility, too, Miranda," Marlon noted.

"What's that?" Miranda asked.

"That the NSA will not be interested in any of this. Because maybe this guy, Joe, we'll call him, was working for the NSA. Just not as an employee."

The phone went silent for a moment. Then, "doing what?" Miranda asked. "Setting a trap for Deren? Planting something on his computer, so it looked like he was stealing data? But why would the NSA do that to one of their own? And what about Paul's computer?"

"Remember, Miranda, don't assume anything," Marlon tutted. "We have no idea what the NSA is doing, or for what reason, about all this or anything else. The proverbial black box, you know."

"And you think Sully's in the dark, too?" Miranda asked.

"Maybe," Marlon answered. "Or maybe he's in on all of it. And is hiding what's really going on from you. From us."

Miranda was quiet for a moment. "I hate to think that of my old friend," she said. "But he does keep reminding me that it's his job to protect the NSA, and that's what he's going to do, regardless."

"I don't know, Miranda," Marlon said. "But keep your wits about you."

Miranda disconnected. Just then, the front door swung open, and Sully strode in. His expression was unreadable, Miranda thought. What was up?

"Schwartz said he didn't buy it," Sully answered.

"You don't sound very surprised," Miranda said, slowly. This was it, she thought. If this was the end of the road for Sully's cooperation with Miranda, Marlon had guessed right. Whatever it was, Sully was in on it.

Sully sat silently. She would let him off the hook, Miranda decided, suddenly. This was all not his problem, after all. She had apparently been pushing him where he wasn't supposed or did not want to go. That wasn't fair to him, she realized.

"Well," she broke the silence, "that's kind of what we've been worried about all along, isn't it?" Miranda asked. "Too much of our story rests on Jessica. And Deren and Paul's claims of innocence, too, when you think about it. Unless you believe in all three, the story sort of falls apart."

But he did not take that bait.

"Yes and no," Sully said. "Yes, if you're telling it to just any Joe Blow. But Schwartz knows me better than to discount my judgment completely. And with any possibility of a trespasser at the NSA on the night of a major data breach, the head of cybersecurity at NSA should be jumping on it. Should be taking whatever steps are necessary to disprove what I've proposed and not blowing me off."

"So, what are you saying?" Miranda asked. "What do you think is going on?"

Sully sighed heavily. "I think it most likely that we've inadvertently stepped into a larger arena. That Schwartz is dealing with a bigger problem, and somehow if he pursues our Joe Smith or re-opens the investigation into the data breach, whatever he's got planned to solve that problem would go awry."

Ah, Miranda thought. He was shutting her out. Just with a different excuse. "Okay," she said, "that's complicated. And totally weird. But so, then, we should just stand back and get out of their way? Even if that means Paul's reputation is destroyed, Deren stays out in the cold, and Jessica stays in her damn wheelchair?" she tried to keep her anger and frustration out of her voice.

"If that were the only possible explanation for Schwartz's reaction, I'd say yes," Sully answered. Miranda glared at him, but when she opened her mouth to respond, Sully cut her off. "But it is possible, just possible, that Schwartz is not on the up-and-up. That he's gone to the dark side."

"Schwartz?" Miranda plopped down suddenly on the sofa. "Your boss? Are you kidding me?"

Sully frowned. "I hate to even think it. But as I told you before, there's a ton of money in cybercrime. Not so much in government service. It's happened before, you know. Too many times. Anyway," Sully rolled his shoulders, relieving the tension, "it's my job to find out. Come on, let's get to work."

"On what?" Miranda asked, bewildered.

Sully explained. Joe Smith might have had invented that one software product and then left the field. Gone off to teach school or something. But maybe not. Maybe he kept coding. Coders usually developed a new program by modifying an existing one. So long as the revised program qualified as "new" within the meaning of the Patent Act, the coder would get a patent on the new program. Because software programs, particularly in the data security area, dated quickly and fell out of use, a good coder would regularly continue this process and end up with multiple patents. An expert in the field could follow the patent trail and find out who owned the most recent patent, and the one covering the products currently in use.

"We'll track Joe's original patent," Sully concluded. "Maybe he's still just a Joe Smith coding away, and we still won't have any way to track him down. But it's also possible that he sold his first patent, or some of his subsequent work, to a legitimate company somewhere along the line. For derivative code, the company will be listed as the inventor, and we can find that company online. We'll need to get Deren in on this. You can help some, but I need another pair of expert eyes to do this quickly."

"Okay, but just a minute," Miranda said. "This Joe guy is a crook, remember? A hacker. If he's selling patents to a legitimate buyer, he can't be using his real identity. So, finding the buyer isn't going to help us find Joe."

"We don't know whether this Joe really hacked the NSA, or not anymore," Sully said impatiently. "Given Schwartz's puzzling reaction to the report I just made, it could be Joe was an NSA plant. Someone at the NSA put him on site to implicate Deren. Or maybe the NSA has turned him. We just don't know."

Sully turned from Miranda, walked into the kitchen to retrieve his laptop, and motioned Miranda to follow him into her office. "In any event, this is all we have right now.

Sully sat his laptop on Miranda's office desk and pulled up the spare chair. "Come on, Miranda, let's go hunting."

A few minutes after they settled into the office, Miranda's phone rang. Sully was talking to Deren on speaker, so Miranda walked out of the office to take the call.

"Father Brennan just called," Marlon said without preliminaries. "Bad news. Terrible news."

"He wasn't able to see her?" Miranda asked, worriedly.

"Oh, he did all aright," Marlon replied. "That's from where the bad news comes. Norma's been accused of money laundering. She'll be deported and handed over to the Mexican police. Tonight."

"Money laundering? Norma?" Miranda clenched her phone hard, hurting her hand. "So this has all been legit? What does Will ..."

"Miranda," Marlon interrupted her. "I don't know anything. Other than what the priest reported. But it sure doesn't look good."

"What happens now?" Miranda asked, mind spinning. It was all just too much to take in.

"Jim went to get the car," Marlon replied. "We're driving to Andrews Air Force Base."

"We?" Miranda asked, surprised. "Who's we? Why Andrews? And what are you planning on doing when you get there?"

"Don't have a clue," Marlon said. "That's about all we figured out from our hours of research. That they would fly her out of Andrews, given the circumstances. Security-wise, none of the other local airports would do. After he talked to Father Brennan, Will announced that he was going to Andrews. He's going to try stopping any ICE vehicle entering the premises, wresting Norma free and driving her to Canada."

"But that's crazy," Miranda protested. "They'll have guns. He could get shot."

"Probably will get shot," Marlon said. "But he's past thinking rationally. Way past. He's on an unstoppable mission."

"So, Will still believe she's innocent?" Miranda asked.

"Not sure. I guess. He hasn't given up, anyway."

"So why again are you with him in this insanity?" Miranda asked angrily.

Marlon sighed heavily. "I couldn't let him go alone. Maybe I can talk to somebody; I don't know. In any event, I'm going along for the brains, and we're bringing Jim for the brawn. In case we need it. And to drive."

"How much time do I have to find a criminal defense lawyer for you guys?" Miranda asked.

"Ha," Marlon said sourly. "Not a time for joking, Miranda," he continued.

"I'm not joking. That's the only outcome I see here, assuming you even find the vehicle she's in."

"I'm going to do my best to keep us on the right side of the law," Marlon said, "but you're right," he sighed. "It can't hurt to be prepared. I don't know how long it'll be," he continued. "We can't actually drive onto Andrews without permission. And they are sure as heck not going to let us in when we ask. 'Excuse me, sir, we want to drive in to highjack an ICE vehicle and snatch a suspected money launderer out of custody.' We'll park as close to the main entrance as we can, then watch and wait."

"I repeat. This is insane, Marlon," Miranda's voice rose. "Get real. You can't do anything for Norma at this point. You can save Will, though. Why don't you drive Will to the ER and have him sedated?" she asked.

"I thought about it," Marlon said. "But I just can't, Miranda. It wouldn't be right. Will needs to know he's done everything he possibly could for his wife. It would wreck him if he doesn't. I'll think of something before somebody pulls a gun on us. I hope."

●　　　●　　　●　　　●

An hour later, Marlon started to complain. "I should have brought my flask," he grumbled.

"Oh, you'd be great help with a martini under your belt," Jim protested. The two were sitting in the front seat of Jim's aging brown Corolla, parked off the access road to the south entrance of Andrews Air Force Base. Marlon had opened the glove box, and the bulb inside it shed a feeble bluish light on their faces.

"But this is so boring," Marlon protested. "We're probably going to sit here all night, and nothing will happen. What are the chances that ICE will go in this way, tonight, with Norma, and we'll actually be able to stop them? Low to none, I'd wager."

"You'd better hope nothing happens," Jim warned. "Will may go crazy, but we won't end up in jail tonight. Or worse."

"I know, I know," Marlon agreed. "I'm just venting. Speaking of Will," Marlon leaned forward and looked out the window past Jim in the driver's seat, "what's he doing now?"

"Burpees," Jim answered promptly.

Marlon shuddered. "Doesn't look like something a human being should be doing," he observed. Marlon had not been near a gym since his mother got him excused from PE in fourth grade because of his asthma. "Borderline," she had protested when Marlon came up with the idea. But she took care of it.

Will had not said much on the drive out. He had sat in the backseat, tight-lipped, white-faced, breathing heavily, fidgeting. After they had agreed, in terse exchanges, where to park, he had gotten out of the car and launched himself into vigorous jumping jacks.

"He probably hasn't been to his gym in a while," Marlon had noted, dryly.

"It's what he needs right now," Jim had responded. "If this goes on much longer, I just may join him."

• • • • •

Sully and Deren, with Miranda attempting to assist, had carefully traced the evolution of the original Joe Smith patent. They had come to the tentative conclusion that Joe's patent was the progenitor of several recent patents, of which the registered owner was Cerberus, Inc.

Under other circumstances, the patent sleuths would have dismissed the link as meaningless. Sully and Deren knew Cerberus was one of the biggest players in the global market for data security software. The company did work for many agencies of the federal government, including the NSA, and would have been thoroughly vetted. No bad apples allowed. The company could simply have purchased Joe's patent rights years ago. Or, if Joe had anything to do with Cerberus, he must be clean.

But these investigators were not sure that Joe was clean. Sully had heard through the grapevine – and NSA's rumor mill was very well-informed – that Steve Schwartz was close with the CEO of Cerberus. Something wasn't adding up. Could their Joe be the CEO of Cerberus?

The team searched the internet for any leads. Other than his name, Mike Danville, they could find very little about the CEO of Cerberus. Nothing on the company website, except flowery encomium obviously written by the marketing department. No bio, no picture. Newspaper articles about the success of Cerberus touting its talented leadership. None written by Dante, however, and no photos from the society pages of the CEO of Cerberus at any charitable event.

"How is that even possible?" Miranda asked. "The CEO of a big, famous company, in a headline-grabbing industry, doesn't make the news? No taped interview? No photo op from Davos?"

Sully shrugged. "If he could fool the best data snoops in the NSA in setting up Deren," he said, "the guy can do about anything, I'd say. Swiped all the stuff from various data repositories, I guess."

"Huh, likes to stay in the shadows, that's for sure," Miranda said, sitting back in her desk chair and stretching.

"Miranda, why don't you take a break," Sully did not even glance up from his laptop. "Give me the room for a minute. I'm going to poke around in some non-public databases. I know you're not going to look over my shoulder or anything, but let's be clean about this."

"Fine by me," she said, standing. "I need a drink."

Sully looked up at her sharply. "Water," she protested. He smiled and went back to work. "And I'll call Marlon," Miranda added as she walked out of the room. "Check on the posse comitatus." Sully chuckled.

•   •   •   •

"Can I put you on speaker?" Marlon asked.

"Sure," Miranda said. "What's going on out there?" her voice sounding unnaturally loud in the shadowy interior of the car.

"Nothing," Marlon said. "Jim and I are sitting here, gossiping. Will's jogging in place outside."

"Any vehicles come by?" Miranda asked.

"Not a one," Marlon answered. "What's happening at your house?"

Miranda explained about the call to Sully's boss and the patent trail. "We've got to dig deeper to find anything about Danville," Miranda concluded. "Sully's surfing around on the Dark Web. I'm about to call a friend of mine who works the late shift at the Post. Ask her to go through archives and see if she can dig up anything on him."

"I've got a picture of him on my phone," Jim said.

"You what?" Miranda, astonished.

It was Jim's turn to explain the catering event last week. About the handsome guy Jim could not keep his eyes off. And who noticed. Who flirted with Jim just a little bit, even though he did not strike Jim as gay. Who laughingly said why didn't Jim just take a picture. So, he did. The conversation about the gates of hell with his colleague. "Couldn't forget that name. Cerberus."

"Text me the picture," Miranda commanded, excitedly. "Now!"

She called back a moment after Jim texted her. "Not him," she wailed. "It's not the bike guy. Dang, I thought we had something. Finally."

"I'm not surprised," Marlon said, calmly, as he put the phone on speaker again. "Think about it, Miranda. Some super-smart hacker isn't going to be running around trespassing at the NSA at night. He would send a flunky. Your bike guy. Joe Smith."

"Huh. Yeah, I see your point," Miranda admitted.

"And it also fits with the connection between the Joe Smith patent and the Cerberus patents that Sully and Deren identified," Marlon continued. "Joe Smith and someone at Cerberus have been working together for a long time."

"Not necessarily the CEO, though," Miranda pointed out.

"No," Marlon said. "But who knows. Can't hurt to show the picture to Deren."

"You're right. I'll get back to you," Miranda said hurriedly and rang off.

Just then, the back door opened, the overhead light flashed brightly on, and Will sat down heavily, sideways, feet dangling out the open door.

"I've been thinking I should call Marla and start talking about what we're going to do if we find out Norma's already in a Mexican jail," he said, woodenly. "My phone's dead, though."

Jim, phone in hand, wordlessly passed it over the seat to Will as Marlon said: "At this time of night?" Marlon glanced at his watch. 11:30.

"Who's the guy?" Will asked automatically, without much interest in his voice. Jim had not closed the text he had sent to Miranda.

"The CEO of Cerberus." Marlon quickly explained what had been going on with the others.

Will, still holding Jim's phone, looked at the screen again. He studied it for a moment, a frown on his face. "I didn't catch it at first," he said slowly, "but I'm pretty sure I know this man. Knew him, that is," he corrected himself, "a long time ago."

Chapter 22

They had both been seniors in high school. In Baltimore. Will was attending a large, public school, and Ed Dante, his opponent's name as Will later found out, was in private school, at Gilman. That was one of the reasons he remembered the incident so well, Will explained. Gilman was the school into which Will's father had tried so hard but failed to get Will. Anyway, it was towards the end of the season. The quarterback for Will's team, Chuck Wilson, was well-known in the state, a rising star being recruited by the big guys like Ohio State and Michigan.

Will stopped and shook his head. "Sorry, guys, more than you needed to know. To get to the point. The center snapped, everyone rushes, and Dante gets to Chuck just as he's about to let one loose. Dante dove at the guy. I heard it, a horrible crunch, a blood-curdling scream, and Chuck dropped like a brick. Dante had taken out his knee. Deliberately. I thought."

Marlon shuddered. "I've always hated that game. But," he continued, "why did you think it was deliberate?"

Will shrugged. "It sure looked like it to me," he answered. "Later," he continued, "I wondered if my reaction was tainted by just that little bit of jealousy. Plus, all the testosterone and anger at what had happened to my buddy, Chuck, of course ..." His voice trailed off. "Just excuses, I guess," he continued. "Because I sure was sorry about it all later."

"Why, what happened?" Jim asked.

"Well, I told my coach," Will said. "He made a big stink with Gilman's people, and I guess Chuck's father did, too. Anyway, Dante was kicked off the team though he denied doing anything wrong. And he hadn't."

"How did you find that out?" Marlon asked.

"That summer, Chuck confessed to me, under penalty of serious injuries permanently inflicted on me by his ex-linebackers if I ever told anybody, that his knee had just snapped. Badly. Dante had hit him fair and square. But Chuck hated to admit his career had been lost due to his own weakness. He didn't want to go out with a whimper. But in battle."

Marlon pointedly and exaggeratedly rolled his eyes.

"I know, I know, ridiculous," Will said. "And all so unfair. To Dante. But that's what happened."

Before anyone could respond, Marlon's phone rang. He answered. "It's he," Miranda said excitedly. "Deren recognized the picture. It was a long time ago, years, but he's sure the CEO of Cerberus is the intern who got kicked out of the law firm. We're ..."

"Deren must be mistaken," Will interrupted her. "That intern was named Richard Dance, remember?"

"Anybody can change his name," Marlon answered, a musing note in his voice. "Ha," Marlon blurted excitedly as he briskly slapped his hand on the dashboard, startling Will and Jim. Corkscrewing his body around in the car to face Will in the back seat, Marlon asked: "Will, when the priest told you about Norma's alleged money laundering, what exactly did he say about it? Did he give you any details about where and how it was supposed to have happened?"

"I ... I don't remember," Will said. "He said 'deported' and 'money laundering,' and my mind went blank."

"Well, call him. Right now," Marlon motioned to Jim's phone, clutched in Will's hand. "I'm guessing old priests don't sleep very much. He'll be up. If not, wake him."

"What are you talking about?" Miranda's voice rose out of Marlon's receiver.

Marlon hit the speaker button and spoke to all of them. "Maybe, just maybe, it's Will who's the real target. Norma was snatched to punish Will."

•   •   •   •   •

At a very early hour Tuesday morning, Sully related what had happened to the Director of the NSA. Will got hold of the priest, who said the authorities told him they had "recent evidence" that Norma was regularly moving money from an account linked to the Sinaloa cartel to a legitimate investment account in Madrid via electronic funds transfer. Other than that short trip to visit her mother, Norma had not been out of the country in months, so the team figured the "planted" evidence – they were working on the assumption that this was another Cerberus strike – likely resided on her home computer. It would be easier to access than the computers at Mid-American Electric, where Norma worked. Marlon convinced Will that he would be doing Norma more good by returning to town to let Sully into their house and give him the password to her computer than waiting around, fruitlessly no doubt, at Andrews.

Sully found the footprint on Norma's computer. And, because he had seen the shadow of this particular culprit three times now, something clicked. Sully realized he had seen this same footprint in another, unexpected place.

On the previous Wednesday, Steve Schwartz had given Sully a thumb drive and instructed him to find the bug in the programs on it. Something one of their consultants had planted for a security exercise, and his security team had missed. Sully had duly examined the drive and identified the bug. And, he now realized, the link between the footprints.

"Schwartz told me that thumb drive came from Cerberus," Sully continued. "Hand-delivered by Danville, in fact. Danville, or whatever his real name is, had a reason, or at least he thought he did, to take revenge on Deren, Paul, and Will, we think. Danville must have hacked the computers of Deren and Paul and Norma, and planted evidence that made his victims look like criminals."

"And you had your suspicions of Schwartz, anyway, and thought he might be in on it somehow," the Director said, nodding his head. "That's why you asked to see me directly."

Sully nodded. "Though I couldn't figure out why he'd have delivered the drive to me if that was the case," he said. "But out of an abundance of caution ..." he trailed off. The Director looked preoccupied.

The Director sat motionless, peering closely at Sully. After a few minutes of silence, Sully started worrying. He had just accused the CEO of a major NSA contractor of illegal hacking. He had expressed doubts about his boss, who reported directly to the Director. Sully had shared information, not quite but close to confidential information with a civilian. He had pursued his investigation of Deren after the NSA closed the matter and Schwartz had ordered him to lay off it.

Suddenly, as though he had just made his decision, the Director spoke. "Good work with the forensics, Sully," he said.

Sully started to relax. Surely a dressing-down would not start with a compliment.

"After all," the Director continued, "we were all fooled. For quite a long time. We should have listened to Agent Pearson. He warned us that he thought we were being misled. Although it all turned out okay in the end, I guess."

The Director explained. A little more than a year ago, they had been approached by Chad, who said he would help the NSA take down his partner, Mike Danville. Chad offered to help uncover evidence implicating Danville in all manner of illegal hacking. The theft of hundreds of millions of euros, yuan, and dollars, all cleverly transformed through money laundering and hidden in tax havens around the world. The unauthorized access to the internal databases of various national security agencies, extraction of sensitive data, and the sale of that data to the highest bidder, whether that be terrorist organizations or rogue states. One of those databases was the NSA's.

"According to Chad, Deren was one of Danville's pawns," the Director continued. "He was unknowingly being used to acquire access to NSA data. Chad went in and plucked out the damning evidence and gave it to us."

Sully frowned. "But that was a year ago," he said. "Why wasn't Deren exonerated? Once you knew?"

"We had evidence, but not enough to go after Danville for the NSA breach," the Director answered. "Besides, we had a lot of his other work to nail, too. We couldn't raise Danville's suspicions. We felt bad about Deren, but it was his job to protect national security. And national security was the larger issue here. We let him take the fall, but we'll make up for it, now."

Sully smiled grimly. "Now. So that means you've nailed Danville."

"Not exactly," the Director replied. "That's where we were all fooled. It never was Danville, whose real name is Dante, by the way. Ed Dante. He officially changed his name. Perfectly legal, you know, unless you're trying to hide a crime. Of which we have no indication. Anyway, Chad showed us the tracks, all right. But it turned out they were leading us to somebody else. The real culprit. The perpetrator of all the criminal activity. Dante and Chad were clean."

"Huh," Sully, surprised. "Who was the real bad guy?"

When the Director told him, Sully blanched. "You've got to be kidding!" he exclaimed. A very famous and wealthy man. Who'd founded what became a multi-billion-dollar software development company, the products of which were downloaded onto most of the computers in the world. Who'd apparently also created a vast and lucrative underground empire, as well.

"But why?" Sully asked. "Why do it?"

The Director shrugged. "It happens," he answered. "I've seen it before. Some very successful people can't stop until they've conquered it all, good and bad. It's the ego, I suppose." Then he held up a warning finger. "Strictly in-house, Sully. Nobody is to know. Even in this building, he's just 'John Doe.' Because if the word got out, it could seriously disrupt the global financial markets. He's going quietly to disappear to an island in the Pacific, supposedly. But that's not where he'll actually be. Not by a very long shot."

"What about Chad?" Sully asked. "And Ed," he added, "because, I assume, they were in it all together. Aren't they in trouble for leading the NSA on this wild goose chase?"

The Director shrugged dismissively, looking at his watch. This would be his last question, Sully could see. "It ended up an incredible coup for the Agency. One we wouldn't have foreseen, and wouldn't have discovered, probably, in a million years. We'll leave it at that."

After the revelations from the Director, Sully put in a quick call to Will, stopped in to see if Schwartz was in and, finding his boss in his office, stopped in for a brief visit. Then Sully went home to get a few hours of sleep, as the others were doing. They all re-grouped in Aaron's offices at 8:30 the next morning, except for Will, who was home with Norma.

Sully disclosed the basics of what had happened, as he had been authorized to do by the Director. Chad and Ed had helped the NSA uncover a major cybercriminal, who'd just been arrested. The identity of the criminal would never be disclosed. He was "John Doe" now and forever. The NSA knew Deren was John Doe's pawn, but not that Paul and Norma were being used, too, until Sully supplied the evidence he and the firm had unearthed. Given the proof that it was John Doe who was using Norma's computer for money laundering and Paul's to commit tax fraud, the Director had made calls. Norma was released and driven home immediately. The U.S. Attorney's office would be lifting Paul's subpoena "right about now," Sully concluded.

"So, we were wrong about all those revenge theories," Aaron said wryly, shaking his head. "Even if Will's and Deren's memory is correct, and this Ed Dante is the same person of whom both accused foul play, as did Paul, Dante didn't have anything to do with what happened to any of them. It was the bad guy. The John Doe. Lesson learned," he continued, "or, I should say, re-learned. We presumed that the first picture to connect all the dots was the right one. Never," he shook his finger, threateningly, "presume."

"Who cares about all that," Miranda said, voice shaking. "What about Jessica? She was an innocent victim here, too, just like Deren and Paul and Norma. And Will. Their lives can easily be fixed. But what about Jessica's?" Miranda asked, angrily.

Sully held up both hands, palms out. "Sorry, Miranda," he said. "I should have told you right away. I understand that's all being worked out."

"What do you …?" Miranda began.

Sully cut her off. "I can't tell you right now. You'll just have to be patient. It's going to be okay. Soon.

Miranda sighed heavily, then subsided. She would trust her friend.

"Does the NSA have any idea why Dante and Chad did all this?" Aaron asked.

"If they do, they didn't tell me," Sully answered.

"Or you can't tell us," Aaron suggested.

Sully just shrugged. In truth, he did not know. The NSA didn't, either. Nor did they understand another part of the puzzle that was Chad and Ed. On Sunday, Chad had delivered a coded message to Schwartz. Chad had said it was the final key to outing Danville. Schwartz had gotten the cryptographers on it immediately, of course. Deciphered, the code led them not to Danville, but to John Doe. And provided the evidence that Paul and Norma, like Deren, were John Doe's pawns. Sully and his friends had just found that evidence a tad bit sooner.

Marlon had been sitting quietly, rhythmically tapping the fingers of one hand on his knee, as though he were stroking the keys on a piano. "I'm puzzled about something," he said. "So, the NSA knew about Deren, but not John Doe's other pawns. Could it really just be a coincidence that two other government agencies, all three independent of each other, looked into Paul's and Norma's computers, respectively, and found evidence of a crime? Furthermore, John Doe probably had thousands, if not millions of such pawns, if he was using personal computers to move so much data around. Could it really just be a coincidence that the three persons who falsely accused Ed Dante ended up as John Doe's pawns?"

Marlon looked around at the others, none of whom said anything. "Somehow, I strongly doubt it," Marlon answered his own question. "It was not a coincidence, that is," he clarified. "I think it's entirely possible that Ed and Chad set up the whole thing," he continued. "I think the two of them took John Doe down, hard, and ensured that the pawns, those pawns that we care about, anyway, took a brief but painful fall."

"Oh, come on, Marlon," Miranda scoffed. "That's way too complicated," she continued. "And how in the world could Ed and Chad have so thoroughly manipulated this major international cybercriminal?"

"Well," Marlon replied, nonchalantly, "in the end, Ed and Chad clearly outplayed him. We can only speculate what all their moves were along the way."

• • • •

It was a stretch for Miranda to head to Charles Street this Thursday morning. Only two days after that crazy night and the office was still off-balance, everybody catching up and trading appointments and covering for Will, who promised to return next week. But it was such a beautiful day, sunny and warm, and Miranda just did not feel like sitting around in an office deposing somebody. Better to be with the kids for a while, anyway.

She had parked and was heading up the sidewalk to the Clinic. The front door opened just as she reached for it and he walked out. Miranda stopped suddenly, stunned.

"This is amazing," Miranda said, excitedly. "We tried to find you, but the NSA wouldn't help, and we didn't have any other leads, and here I just bump into you ..." she said in a rush, stopping suddenly. "But wait a minute," she continued more slowly, "What in the world are you doing here?"

"I ... I work here," Chad answered. "Volunteer, that is. I haven't been in a couple of years, but I used to volunteer all the time," Chad explained. "My sister had cerebral palsy. I've always loved working with the little ones. That's what you're doing here, too, right?" he asked.

Miranda nodded. "You know, I have a lot of other questions, too," she began, as Chad cut her off.

"Can't tell you anything," he said, but gently, as he touched her lightly on the arm and turned her around, away from the door. "Top secret," he said, a smile in his voice. "Sit for a minute," he continued, pointing her towards the wooden bench on its concrete pedestal beside the sidewalk.

Miranda did as she was told. For some reason, he seemed perfectly normal to her. Not a super-sleuth with mysterious motives and complicated means. A little older than she. Not bad looking, though. They sat. She wondered about all this hush-hush, though.

"Is that just an excuse?" she asked. "It's not that you can't tell me, but you just won't?"

"Ahh, what does it matter," Chad drawled lazily.

"I suppose it doesn't," Miranda nodded. "Anyway," she continued energetically, "we all want to thank you properly. Jessica, in particular, of course. For all the money that will cover the treatment and whatever Jessica will need to live as normal a life as possible if the treatment doesn't work out. We're planning that it will, of course," Miranda interrupted her excited rambling to take a deep breath. "Jessica's already gone to the Caymans. But before she left, she made me promise I'd keep trying to find you."

Chad waved his hand at her, dismissively. "Yeah, I knew she was gone," he drawled. "It had to be done, Miranda. Everything went just as planned, except for Jessica. So as soon as we could, we fixed that, too. As much as we could." He leaned back on the bench and stretched out his legs. "It's a beautiful day, isn't it?"

"Yes, it is that," Miranda answered as she sat back on the warm wooden bench. He knew her name, she thought, sleepily. Remembered it from all those years ago? Seemed doubtful. Well, the NSA knew it. Probably passed it on to Chad. Abruptly, she sat up straight. But Jessica?

"How did you know?" she asked. "That Jessica was gone?"

Chad considered it briefly. Considered telling her that they had bugged her phone. To keep track of Miranda and her team's plays in the game. She seemed such a nice person. Smart, too. He knew she would be dismayed, even though it had been for a just cause. Someday, he thought. Just not today.

"The NSA knows everything," he finally said, smiling broadly.

Cryptic, Miranda thought. But he did have a lovely smile. She smiled, too.

Acknowledgements

Many thanks to our families and friends for their enthusiasm for our project and unflagging support, and for all their suggestions and advice on technical issues. A special thanks to our first readers: Nancy Hite, Carol Lucy, Ann Riedy, and Amy Sage Webb.

About the Authors

Marian K. Riedy obtained her law degree from Harvard Law School, practiced as a civil litigator for many years, and is currently an associate professor. She is a distance runner; plays tennis, handball, and golf; enjoys the opera and symphony; has master points in bridge; and always has a few new books to read on her Kindle.

Tanja Steigner graduated from the University of South Florida with a Ph.D. in finance. While her primary focus is scholarly articles on corporate finance, tax evasion, and Fintech, she also enjoys regular forays into the realm of fiction. Above all, she is a devoted wife and mother, who loves spending free time with her family.

Note from the Authors

Word-of-mouth is crucial for any author to succeed. If you enjoyed the book, please leave a review online—anywhere you are able. Even if it's just a sentence or two. It would make all the difference and would be very much appreciated.

Thanks!
Marian & Tanja

Thank you so much for reading one of our **Thrillers**.

If you enjoyed our book, please check out our recommended title for your next great read!

The Tracker by John Hunt

"A dark thriller that draws the reader in." –*Morning Bulletin*

"I never want to hear mention of bolt-cutters, a live rat and a bucket in the same sentence again. EVER." –*Ginger Nuts of Horror*